The Final
Unfinished Voyage
of Jack Aubrey

Patrick O'Brian was, until his death in 2000, the author of the acclaimed Aubrey-Maturin novels and the biographer of Joseph Banks and Picasso. He also wrote other novels including *Testimonies*, and many short stories. In 1995 he was the first recipient of the Heywood Hill Prize for a lifetime's contribution to literature. In the same year he was awarded the CBE. In 1997 he received an honorary doctorate of letters from Trinity College, Dublin. In 2003, his Aubrey novels were taken to the big screen by the film director Peter Weir with the blockbuster and critically acclaimed *Master and Commander: The Far Side of the World*. He died in Dublin in January 2000.

The Works of Patrick O'Brian

PATRICK O'BRIAN

The Final
Unfinished Voyage
of Jack Aubrey

*Including facsimile of
the manuscript*

HarperCollins*Publishers*

HarperCollins*Publishers*
77–85 Fulham Palace Road,
Hammersmith, London W6 8JB
www.harpercollins.co.uk

This edition published by HarperCollins 2005

First published by HarperCollins*Publishers* 2004
1 3 5 7 9 8 6 4 2

A catalogue record for this book
is available from the British Library

ISBN 0 00 719470 6

Printed and bound in Thailand
by Imago

NOTE

When Patrick O'Brian died in early January 2000, he left 65 handwritten pages of the untitled twenty-first novel in the Aubrey/Maturin series. He had also begun typing the same material and had made revisions to the typescript.

The printed version presented here follows the author's revised typescript, with the correction of a few obvious omissions and errors of spelling. But it is not to be supposed that these pages are exactly as O'Brian would have wanted them to be in a final draft, or had he seen proofs of his book. There are occasional word repetitions and rhyming echoes that he would surely have caught on subsequent readings. The typescript ends in mid-sentence (page 110), and chapter 3 continues—without conclusion—in O'Brian's own hand. The facsimile pages include such wonderful curiosities as O'Brian's sketch of the seating arrangements for a dinner party, and the reader is granted a last, intimate glimpse of this extraordinary writer practising his craft.

FOREWORD

by William Waldegrave

THIS BOOK CONTAINS a fragment. It is the beginning of a beginning of Patrick O'Brian's twenty-first novel, left uncompleted at his death. We do not know the shape of the story he had planned; he left no outline or sketch. We do not have a finished version of any of the three chapters, the manuscript and typescript versions of which are reproduced here. Much further perfectionist, painstaking work would have gone on before that eagle eye would have been satisfied.

But what we do have is of extraordinary interest to lovers of O'Brian's magnificent naval series. The personal glimpse we get of this intensely private man at work is both moving and impressive. We see a master craftsman, still in full possession of his craft, pressing on, even in old age, with the same dedication and courage which, through a long life containing many set-backs and vicissitudes, brought him in the end to fame and success.

It is rather as if we had opened the door to the studio of a great painter and found that he had left a canvas on the easel, almost entirely untouched – this is not one of those painters who sketch in the whole and then overpaint – but with one corner glowing with some fine colours. Some detail is already there, worked up; some brush strokes are clearly sketched, to be revisited; others point to the architecture of the whole and give an inkling of what the completed structure might have looked like.

Most touchingly, as in the margins of Edward Lear watercolours, we also find personal little notes and memoranda written to himself: there he is, suddenly, Patrick O'Brian himself, rubbing shoulders on the page with Jack Aubrey and Stephen Maturin in the same fine handwriting.

Uncovering the way in which O'Brian writes is a task for the professional literary scholar, not for me. But, looking at these manuscript pages, and at the typescript, certain conclusions seem to suggest themselves.

First, O'Brian seems to work at several levels in terms of completeness at the same time. On one level, the frontier of the story is pushed forward boldly, with a broad brush – surely leaving behind gaps for later infilling. Thus we sweep across the southern Atlantic from the Strait of Magellan to the coast of South Africa, providing a structure for the first quarter or so of the book in outline, but leaving plenty of room for the insertion not only of detail but also, and without difficulty, of quite substantial further episodes.

Then, at another level of finish, there are episodes well worked up and broadly complete, like the meeting between Jack and his black papal nuncio son, Sam, in Buenos Aires. Here, more polishing undoubtedly would have been done, but I would be surprised if anything much would have changed.

Finally, there are paragraphs not only worked up but perfect and complete. Take the moment – so central to Jack's life-long ambition – when his rear-admiral's flag is finally broken out at the mizzen of his own first flagship:

'The folded bundle soared aloft, followed with the utmost concentration by all hands: at exactly the right moment, the exact height to an inch, the coxswain snapped the tie and the rear-admiral's blue flag streamed out bravely in the wind, instantly greeted by the first of thirteen solemn guns, enormously loud, salutes from all the members of the blue squadron, distant cheering from *Surprise* and clouds of wheeling, discontented gulls.'

This seems to me perfect, but it has taken many careful revisions to achieve, with the seagulls, in particular, overpainted again and again: 'uneasy', 'complaining', 'querulous' are all tried for size, but to my ear the typescript version is best and would surely have remained.

So that square inch or two of the canvas is finished, almost varnished, while the majority remains quite blank, and surrounding areas are only sketched and touched in.

If I am right, and O'Brian is pushing forward the story at different levels of completeness at the same time, with almost everything subject to revision, and with the possibility of considerable insertions (these unfinished chapters are, after all, a good deal shorter than most of those in the completed books), it is worth pausing for a moment on the themes which these early chapters promise. We can allow ourselves the luxury of dreaming about what might have been the elements of this story.

Some are well signalled. Lord Leyton is obviously going to be a choleric and difficult commander-in-chief. If Jack could lose his temper so dangerously all those years before in the Admiralty boardroom with Lord St Vincent himself, how much more danger is there of ructions and rows with Lord Leyton?

Then there is Maturin's flowering relationship with the intelligent, long-legged naturalist Christine: is Maturin at last to find unclouded happiness? The hope inclines one to make the sign against the evil eye, sharing the superstition of the sailors; so often O'Brian, who in so many ways models Maturin closely upon himself, seems to inflict disaster on his fictional alter ego.

And we are on the way to the Cape, taken not so long ago from the Dutch, and then, as now, a hotbed of complex politics and, of course, a paradise for the botanist and naturalist. I am sure Stephen would have encountered an oryx, at least. The fleet is to be based at the Cape to protect the India and China trade: pirates, opium and perhaps Burmese adventures lie without too much anachronism to the east.

But to the west lies one place about which surely we are meant to hear more, whether on the way to the Cape or later: St Helena. Can we really have Jack and Stephen in range of the imprisoned Napoleon without some encounter? Indeed, Lord Leyton announces that he will interview the unfortunate Emperor and explain to him how he might have won the battle of Waterloo.

What is more, O'Brian, like Marryat and Forester before him, borrows freely from the extraordinary career of Thomas Cochrane, Lord Dundonald, the greatest frigate captain of the age. Cochrane went to Chile and Brazil for the same purpose as did Aubrey in *Blue at the Mizzen*, and their adventures are not dissimilar. Cochrane never actually called on Napoleon (who called him 'that sea wolf') but he planned to do so,

and in the most extraordinary circumstances. He concocted a harebrained scheme for rescuing the great man and carrying him off to Brazil, there to install him as the Emperor of South America, a scheme which, not surprisingly, was never brought to fruition (though history would have been much more fun if it had been).

While Cochrane was a radical, who still admired Napoleon for his revolutionary youth, Jack Aubrey is a Tory through and through, and Maturin hates Napoleon, whose secret police have tortured him, and considers him a tyrant who has destroyed the small nations of Europe. No scheme of Cochrane's type would have been entertained for a moment on board HMS *Suffolk*. But I still cannot imagine that we should not have had some encounter. We will never know.

The fascination of these pages lies in the privilege they give us of seeing, most intimately, the master at work. There is sadness in it: his beloved wife Mary had died, and she was the background to the whole of his mature writing life. She typed his manuscripts and, I suspect, discussed them with him. Without Mary, he could not manage the house in French Catalan Collioure; so he was no longer working in the familiar cave-like writing-room under the house that he had himself largely designed and built, with everything to hand exactly where he wanted it.

We see him now struggling to keep at least two manuscript versions in order, clearly doing his own typing, somewhat erratically, and sometimes apparently composing directly onto the typewriter as well as with the pen. Some manuscript pages are fair copies, in a strong clear hand, others are not. There are overlapping pages, repetitions, excisions, notes to himself. There is a considerable episode (the duel which Maturin fights) which is not yet in the typescript at all. There are distressing notes at the end where he thinks he has lost some of chapter three (and suspects – in a phrase that is pure Maturin – 'a malignant hand'). Evidently, it was found again, because here we have it with the table plan for Lord Leyton's dinner in the margin, just as he describes.

It is impossible not to be moved by the courage and the anxiety of O'Brian, now an old man and alone (though, to his infinite pleasure, pride and gratitude, sheltered and honoured by Trinity College, Dublin), as he tries to keep his pages in order, writes notes about the need for more ink-cartridges for his pen, and on one page writes, very small, 'I am absurdly sleepy', in the way that medieval scribes sometimes wrote comments about the weather or their health in the margins of the illuminated manuscripts on which they were working.

It is the courage that is most striking: the discipline, the will. He has no intention of retiring or throwing in the towel. I leave it to the reader to judge, but out of these fragments, these very fragmentary fragments, I have no doubt that another fine story would have been built if he had had time.

Part of the strength, it might seem, flows back from the very characters he has himself created. It is as if these old friends offer their author comfort. Not for him the prickly and hostile relationship between Conan Doyle and Sherlock Holmes. O'Brian does not want to push Aubrey or Maturin over the Reichenbach falls in order to free himself of their tyranny, as Conan Doyle (unsuccessfully) did Holmes, in order to return the spotlight to such books as *The White Company* which he thought his best.

On the contrary, O'Brian loves Aubrey, and is increasingly indistinguishable from Maturin who loves Aubrey too. It is impossible for those of us who were lucky enough to know him not to hear O'Brian in every sentence of Maturin – and vice versa. Such speculation is dangerous, but perhaps we can catch a faint echo, in the opening passage of chapter one, where Maturin struggles with paper and pens and fusses about completing a letter to Christine, of O'Brian's own efforts to restore order to his recalcitrant ring-binders. But we should be careful: O'Brian, like all great artists had a powerful and concentrated will, and there was no more self-pity in him than there is in Maturin.

Nevertheless, in these pages it is perhaps not too fanciful to imagine that O'Brian has accorded himself the comfort of slipping into the world he has created in order to take refuge among his characters: gossiping with them about old adventures and planning out with them new stories. Sitting with them, perhaps, in the new rear-admiral's great cabin over a bottle or two of that lovely claret he delighted to pretend was 'un petit vin de famille' – Chateau Haut Brion.

I have said that it seems to my unprofessional eye that what we read here is not a first or a second draft of something which would necessarily remain in this shape, awaiting only polishing. Rather, if I am right, we have some finished paragraphs set in a sketched structure which itself might well have been revisited (to accommodate Napoleon, for example), expanded, contracted, pushed about until he had his twelve or fourteen chapters roughed in, and then all to be redone again to the level of perfectionism which would have satisfied him. To return to my analogy of the painter, reading these pages is like watching the master getting out his brushes, mixing his colours, preparing his canvas, starting to paint one part of his great design, sketching a little, revisiting and working up some corner which has already gone well.

It is not like uncovering one perfect incomplete section cut from a finished canvas; we should not judge it like that; but characteristic brush strokes of the master are there. I delight in the unexpected adjectives, which hint at other little stories or digressions which could be followed up if you so wished: 'improbable quantities of port'; a 'shameless wombat'. I love the unexplained mystery of the obscurely strewn drowned dogs, not to mention the cabbage-selling werewolf on page 22. Sometimes you can see a tiny change made that transforms the first sketch into the finished O'Brian: how much better surely is 'seventy of the finest guinea pigs' than the first draft's 'some …' And how typical of O'Brian to enjoy the somewhat shocking fact (to English sensibilities at least) that in parts of Latin America our children's furry friends are indeed a delicacy on which one dines.

Imagine ourselves as literary scholars of the thirty-first century, experts in textual reconstruction. All O'Brian's completed books have been lost like the scrolls of Sappho's lyric poetry in some future equivalent of the Christian burning of the library of Alexandria or the Crusader sacking of Byzantium. By chance, only this book has survived. We future scholars would be intrigued, and a little puzzled. How could so many first-rank critics and so many excellent fellow novelists (their reviews have somehow survived my putative literary holocaust) have acclaimed O'Brian as the greatest historical novelist of his age? Or, as some would have it, of any age?

At first, we would find it hard to understand. But then the best of us, some future TJ Binyon or John Bailey, would get it. They would draw attention to the completed and polished paragraphs, where we have them, and ask us to imagine a whole book written in such elegant, exact and evocative prose – rather as we take the few lines we have left of Sappho and imagine the lost volumes of her poetry.

They would see at once the depth of learning – about history, the Royal Navy of the time, the scientific knowledge of the time (particularly natural history, medicine and astronomy) – worn so lightly but deployed so securely. (See how he grounds his description of the birds of the Strait of Magellan on Darwin himself in the note to the manuscript on page 15.)

They would grasp at once the sense of historical drama, the sweep of great events in the background, setting off the passionate commitment to the individuality of the *dramatis personae* in the foreground.

They would understand the sympathy for the close-knit community of a sailing warship – that mixture of camaraderie and claustrophobia caught so brilliantly by Peter Weir's film *Master and Commander: the Far Side of the World*.

They would see the humour just under the surface of so much of the writing: the sort of joke implied by the 'almost' in the Argentine official's suspicions that these northerners are 'given to cursing the Holy Father almost every day.' They would suspect that O'Brian was a writer who could make us laugh as well as cry.

They would not be able to imagine the full riches from this fragment, of course, any more than we can imagine everything that lay behind Sappho's reputation in antiquity from the bits and pieces which have survived. Nor would they be able to imagine the sheer tension of the sea chases in the completed books – page after page as that relentless Dutchman pursues them through the mountainous seas of the roaring forties in *Desolation Island*.

Perhaps, brought up short, for example, by that werewolf, they might have wondered about O'Brian's interest in taking us down strange, almost ghostly, unexpected pathways of the imagination – and noted the contrast between those surreal and beautiful episodes and the robust realism of his picture of life in the pubs and clubs of a smelly and raucous Regency England. But surely, no one would guess quite the otherworldly and lyrical beauty of the picture he conjures of a Buddhist Garden of Eden, in which live the charming orang-utans of *The Thirteen Gun Salute* – a picture, O'Brian once told me, which was based on nothing other than his pure and extraordinary imagination.

They would not be able to predict the brilliance of the sustained comic writing of passages like the foxhunt in *Master and Commander*, where both Aubrey and Maturin first meet Diana (the oxen nearly cutting a caper of their own at the end of that episode are my favourite oxen in literature).

Nothing yet written in the first workings for the twenty-first book would have shown them O'Brian's heart-wrenching capacity to depict friendship under the extreme pressures of battle, storm, triumph, disaster and the rivalries of love which makes the Aubrey–Maturin relationship one of the great creations of literature.

However, I would be willing to bet that plenty of these things and many others

which we, the readers who do have access to those other twenty finished books, know so well, would also have been there in number twenty-one if it had been finished,

So it is fitting, as we close this last book, to give thanks for what Patrick O'Brian did complete and to celebrate a magnificent life's work. From the extraordinary juvenile books, through *Testimonies* and the short stories, to the translations, the wonderful Picasso biography, *Joseph Banks*, the two Anson novels (the first of which is as good as anything he wrote) and then to the crowning achievement of the twenty completed Aubrey–Maturin novels, it is a body of work to stand comparison with any.

In the margin of the manuscript on page 105, he notes down words which show he is thinking about Macbeth's famous speech on death and reputation:

> Tomorrow, and tomorrow and tomorrow,
> Creeps in this petty pace from day to day,
> To the last syllable of recorded time;
> And all our yesterdays have lighted fools
> The way to dusty death …

But, on the evidence of this last fragment of O'Brian, he was not surrendering, not giving up the ghost. He had another book to write, or perhaps two. He had his craft, his skill, his scholarship, his imagination, his humour, his strong sense of honour – and his courage. When he thinks he has lost much of what he has written, he writes to himself on the last page that he may be able to rebuild the missing pages, but 'I shall have tea first and concentrate what wits I still possess.'

Complex and subtle he was: but he was no despairing Macbeth. Rather he was like the aged Ulysses, Aubrey's ultimate literary forebear, in Tennyson's poem, setting off once again with undaunted spirit into the unknown:

> Old age hath yet his honour and his toil;
> Death closes all: but something ere the end
> Some work of noble note may yet be done,
> Not unbecoming men that strove with Gods …

I hope that last tea was a good one – like the one the three little girls sought on page 88, 'with cake or at least muffin.'

Never did a writer deserve it more, nor the gratitude and affection of his readers throughout the world.

The Final
Unfinished Voyage
of Jack Aubrey

CHAPTER ONE

STEPHEN MATURIN squared up to his writing-desk once more: he had been called away to attend to one of the ship's boys who in the lightness of his heart had contrived to stun himself in the foretop by taking the maul from its place, tossing it to a considerable height and so misjudging the revolutions as it fell that the massive head struck him down, speechless and unnaturally pale. Stephen dressed the wound, such as it was (more bruise than blood and no bone broken) and said to his loblolly-boy, 'Tell Dr Jacob, when he comes back, that this boy is to have no grog for the next three days, and tomorrow he may keep his hammock.' Dr Jacob, the surgeon's mate, was away visiting friends aboard the frigate's tender, the rapid and windwardly Chesapeake schooner *Ringle*, and Stephen glanced in her direction, fine on the starboard bow, before going down from the brilliance of noon to the comparatively sombre cabin that he shared with Captain Aubrey.

He had already written *My dear Christine* before he was called away, and he had dated the letter *Surprise, at sea, in Magellan's Strait*. At his first sitting down he had meant to tell her, with what skill he could command, of the extraordinary beauty of the weather and of the Strait, generally so forbidding: he should certainly have spoken of the favourable wind that had allowed them to keep topgallantsails abroad ever since the morning watch; but above all he should have dwelt upon the happiness that filled the ship, homeward bound after a very long, arduous and most uncommonly dangerous voyage, a well-found ship commanded by a right seaman, a well-liked, deeply-respected fighting captain who, moreover, was soon to hoist his flag. There was no secret about this: Jack Aubrey's first unrestrained cries of delight on receipt of the blessed order had not escaped his steward nor anyone else within a range of twenty yards: nor had the unwonted floods of rum, the feasts in cabin, gunroom and midshipmen's

Chapter I

Stephen Maturin squared up to his writing desk once again: he had been called away to attend to one of the ship's boys, who had contrived to skin himself in the foretop by taking the mail from its place, forcing it to a considerable height and so misjudging the revolutions as it fell that the massive dead struck him down, speechless and unnaturally pale. Stephen dressed the wound, such as it was (more bruise than blood and no bone broken) and said to his loblolly-boy, 'Poll, tell Dr Jacob, when he comes back, that this boy is to have no grog for the next three days, and tomorrow he may keep his hammock.' Dr Jacob, the surgeon's mate, was away visiting friends aboard the frigate's tender, that rapid and windwardly Chesapeake schooner Ringle, and Stephen glanced in her direction, from the starboard bow, before going down from the brilliance of noon to the comparatively somber cabin which he shared with Jack Aubrey.

He had already written My dear Christine before he was called away, and he had dated the letter Surprise, at sea, in Magellan's Strait. At his first sitting down he had meant to tell her, with what skill he could command, of the extraordinary beauty of the weather, and of the strait, ordinarily so forbidding: he should certainly have spoken of the favourable wind that had allowed them to keep topgallantsails abroad ever since the morning watch; but above all he should have dwelt upon the happiness that filled the ship, homeward bound after a long, arduous and most uncommonly dangerous voyage, a well-found ship commanded by a right seaman, a well-liked, deeply respected fighting Captain who, moreover, was soon to hoist his flag. There was no secret about this: Captain Aubrey's first inarticulate cries of delight had not escaped his steward or anyone else within a range of twenty yards; nor had the if unwonted floods of rum, the feasts in cabin, gunroom and midshipmen's

on receipt of the blessed signal / message

berth; and the sacred blue flag itself, the mark of a rear-admiral, lay openly on the fo'c'sle, shaded from too fierce a sun, from untimely drops of spray, by an awning, the sailmaker and his mates, the ship's tailor and his, titivating it with minute stitches, while every hand aboard added half an inch of seam around its ample verge. It was considered the handsomest ensign in the service.

But for the moment the flag was absent from Stephen's mind: indeed the mind itself was in a singular state of absence, hesitation, even stupidity. Before being called to the wretched boy, he had known at least the general trend of the passages that were to follow the words that lay there before him; but now he was filled with doubt, and to give his wits time to settle and clarify he mended his pen, clipping its tip with a minute pair of metal jaws made for the purpose and trimming the sides with a lancet capable of splitting hairs.

Yet the right free, easy, candid expressions would not come, though the Christine in question was very dear to him: Stephen had long practised medicine, a calling in which discretion is often of great importance; but for an even longer time, if time is to be measured by stress, he had been an intelligence-agent, and here discretion was of the very essence, since an unguarded word or step might lead to the agent's death and to the death, the often hideous death, of his friends and the destruction of their cause.

He sat down, his expression still tolerably blank: he was a lean, middle-sized man, unremarkable, of mixed Catalan and Irish origin; but it was the tropical sun and the sea-air that accounted for his dark complexion, not any mixture of Moorish blood, for although his birth was illegitimate (which weighed upon him) his ancestors had been Christians time out of mind. A man of something less than forty, though he looked older as his mind wrestled with the difficulties of giving the intelligent woman he longed to marry a coherent, plausible account of the *Surprise*'s activities and of her present return, mission accomplished: for as soon as Captain Aubrey joined the South African squadron in the River Plate, going aboard HMS *Suffolk*, taking command of her and hoisting or causing to be hoisted the flag, blue at the mizzen, her act would turn him into that glorious creature a rear-admiral,

berth; and the sacred blue flag itself lay openly on the forecastle, shaded from too fierce a sun, from untimely drops of spray, by an awning, the sailmaker and his mates, the ship's tailor and his, titivating it with minute stitches, while every hand aboard added half an inch of the finest seam around its ample verge. It was considered the handsomest ensign in the service.

But for the moment the flag was ~~was~~ absent from Stephen's mind; indeed the mind itself was in a singular state of absence, hesitation, even stupidity. Before being called to that wretched boy he had known the general trend of the ~~words~~ being that were to follow the words that lay there before him, but now he was filled with doubt and to give his wits to time to settle and clarify he mended his pen, chipping its end with a minute pair of metal jaws made for the purpose and trimming its sides with a lancet capable of splitting a hairs.

Yet the right free, easy, candid expressions would not come, though the Christine in question was very dear to him; Stephen had long practised medicine, a calling in which discretion is often of great importance; but for an even longer time, if time is to be measured by slices, he had been an intelligence agent, and here discretion was of the very essence, since an unguarded/slip might lead to the agent's death and the death, the often hideous death, of his friends and the destruction of their cause.

He sat down, his expression still tolerably blank: he was a lean, middle-sized man, unremarkable, of mixed Catalan and Irish origin, but it was the tropical sun and the sea-air that accounted for his dark complexion not any mixture of Moorish blood; for although his birth was illegitimate (which weighed upon him) his ancestors had been Christians time out of mind. A man of something less than forty, though he looked older as his mind wrestled with the difficulties of giving the intelligent woman he longed to marry a coherent, plausible account of the Surprise's activities and of her present return, mission accomplished: for when Captain Aubrey joined the South African squadron in the River Plate, going aboard HMS Suffolk, taking command of her and hoisting ~~or causing it to be~~ hoisted his flag, blue at the mizzen, that would turn him into that glorious creature a rear-admiral.

fo'c'sle

leant

word or

?

the likelihood, the virtual certainty, was that *Surprise* should return to England, carrying Jack Aubrey's official dispatch, two young men who were to pass for lieutenant and a great number of papers and certificates from the bosun, carpenter, gunner and purser justifying the expenditure or replacement of almost every item in the ship's unbelievably complex gear, furnishings and supplies, from pistol-flints to great round-shot and innumerable blocks. There was also a flat, factual, unadorned account of the *Surprise's* meetings with the Chilean authorities and of her proceedings, together with volume after volume of her activity in charting and surveying the South American islands and coasts.

She was one of the smaller frigates, carrying no more than 28 great guns, and although in the right hands she was an outstanding sailer she had been sold out of the service when heavier craft were built and Stephen had bought her: so there she was, eminently seaworthy and available for hire to the Hydrographical Service of the Admiralty once Napoleon had been dealt with and the western world was at something like peace.

Her ostensible function was to survey and chart the little-known coasts and innumerable islands of the recently independent republic of Chile and to help form its navy, training the young officers. All this was perfectly avowable and even praiseworthy, but the voyage had other aspects that were never distinctly laid down in written orders but that were implied and understood on either side: and here total candour was wholly out of the question, so that Stephen's letter home could obviously not be all he wished.

In the first place, through Stephen's innumerable connexions, Jack had been appointed commander-in-chief of the Chilean navy as well as Admiralty hydrographer; but the frigate's voyage had been slow (very foul weather south of the Horn) and when she reached Chile she found that the situation had changed remarkably. Apart from anything else she was met with a bewildering number of juntas, of more or less independent governing bodies belonging to widely differing political parties, one of which had appointed its own commander-in-chief though all were

& receipts
& certificates from the boom. comptroller, governor and prices)

①

the likelihood, the virtual certainty, was that the _Surprise_ should ~~go~~ return

Ye England

home, carrying Jack Aubrey's official despatch, letters home from those
who could write, two young men who were to pass for lieutenants, and a
great number of papers that justified the expenditure or replacement of the
ship's unbelievably complex ~~and important~~ gear: furnishings and supplies from
pistol flints to great roundshot & innumerable blocks. There was also a flat,

~~meadows~~
unadorned

factual, ~~account~~ day-by-day account of the _Surprise_'s meetings with the Chilean
authorities and of her proceedings.

~~She had arrived in Chile after a long and arduous voyage round
the Horn~~ She was one of the smaller frigates, carrying no more than
28 great guns, and although in the right hands she were a most
outstanding sailor she had been sold out of the service when the heavier
craft were built and Stephen had bought her, so there she was, eminently
seaworthy and available for hire to the Hydrographical Service of the
Admiralty once Napoleon had been dealt with and the western world
was at something like peace

Her ostensible function was to survey and chart the little-known
coasts and innumerable islands of ~~the~~ the recently independent republic
of Chile and to help form ~~the~~ its navy, training the young officers
All this was perfectly avowable and even praiseworthy, but the
voyage had other aspects that were never distinctly laid down,
in written orders but that were implied and understood on both sides –
and her total candour was wholly out of the question, so that
Stephen's letter home could obviously not be all he wished

In the first place, through Stephen's innumerable connexions Jack
had been appointed commander-in-chief of the Chilean navy as
well as Admiralty hydrographer, but the frigate's voyage ~~to~~ had
been slow and when she reached Chile she found that the situation
had changed remarkably. Apart ~~from~~ anything else she met with
a bewildering number of juntas, of more or less independent
governing bodies belonging to wholly differing political parties, one
of which had appointed its own commander-in-chief though all were

alarmed, surprised, displeased

obsessed by the fear of a Peruvian invasion by land or sea or both: Peru was still ruled by the Spanish king's viceroy in Lima, and it still possessed a powerful, well-trained navy.

After a very great number of vicissitudes, changes of ministry and so on it appeared to Jack that since his main duty, often expressed in London but never committed to writing, was to preserve the independent Chilean republic, the best way of doing so and at the same time of protecting his beloved infant Chilean navy was to attack the Peruvians in their port of Callao and if possible to cut out their powerful frigate *Esmeralda*, the heaviest, best-armed man-of-war on the Pacific coast of America. This he did with extraordinary success, at the risk of his life; and he brought the *Esmeralda* back to Valparaiso. He was much flattered and caressed, but later he was treated very shabbily indeed: his men were not paid, they were denied their prize-money from various sources, and upon some pretext his ship was threatened with impoundment. Yet though Jack sometimes behaved like a simpleton by land, and though he was often swindled ashore, he was sea-wise, and having provisioned and stored his ship with the basic supplies needed to carry her at least to some port in the Argentine, he handed the Chileans an ultimatum: either his men must have their due by a given date or he should sail away. They were not paid, and he did sail away. Yet although the *Surprise*'s voyage had something of the appearance of a failure, in fact the Spanish hold on South America was broken: and although this had not been the Admiralty's direct order, the result gave immense satisfaction in the proper

[N.B.: *The facsimile page opposite and the following one mostly overlap. See O'Brian's note in the margin.*]

that *Surprise*, a former Royal Naval frigate, sold out of the service put., bought by Stephen himself, and for this ocean sailing as a hired Surveying hydrographical vessel with the function of laying down the ill-charted coasts and islands of the recently independent republics of Chile and of helping to form the new Chilean navy. Training the young officers ◦ The *Surprise* she had was met with a bewildering number of more or less governing bodies of widely differing political parties, and with the ever-present threat threat of Peruvian invasion by land or sea or both — Peru at that time still being ruled from Lima by the Spanish King's viceroy and still possessed a powerful fully-trained navy.

After a very great number of vicissitudes, changes of government and so on it appeared to Jack Aubrey that — who had had never a means c but but precarious little in the way of formal, exact written instructions. — that the ❘ best way of preserving the Chilean republic and above all of protecting his beloved infant Chilean navy was to attack the Peruvians in their port of Callao and if possible to cut out their big frigate, the heaviest, best-armed man-of-war on the Pacific coast of America. — This he did with extraordinary success. Though (at the risk of his life), bringing the big Esmeralda's into Valparaiso. But although he was very much flattered and caressed, he was treated very shockingly: his men were not paid: they were denied their prize-money from various sources: and upon some pretext that his ship was threatened with impoundment. But though Jack was not always overly some time behaved truth a Simpleton by land, and though he was often swindled ashore, he was sea-wise, and having provisioned and stored his ship with everything needed enough to carry her home, he issued an ultimatum to the Chileans: either his men must have their due by a given date or he should sail away. They were not paid, and he did sail away. Yet although the *Surprise*'s voyage something of had the appearance of a failure, in fact the Spanish hold in South America were broken; and although this had not been the Admiralty's direct order, the result gave great pleasure in the right quarters

I think that in typing I confused their two pages. For the moment I shall leave them. Since I want to clear it again — everything after will be there

quarters.

Furthermore Jack had on board a singularly amiable and gifted young man, the unacknowledged but much beloved illegitimate son of Prince William, Admiral the Duke of Clarence, a zealous sailor and almost certain to be king after his brother's death. Clarence had a great respect for Captain Aubrey (some of Jack's actions were indeed

obsessed by the fear of a Peruvian invasion by land or sea or both: Peru
was still ruled by the Spanish King's viceroy in Lima, and it still possessed
a powerful, well-trained navy.

After a very great number of vicissitudes, changes of ministers,
and so on it appeared in fact that since his main duty, often expressed
in London but never committed to writing, was to preserve the ~~independent~~ Chilean
republic, the best way of doing so and at the same time of protecting
his beloved infant Chilean navy was to attack the Peruvians in their
port of Callao and if possible to cut out their big frigate Esmeralda,
far heaviest, best-armed man-of-war on the Pacific coast of America.
This he did with extraordinary success, at the risk of his life; and he
brought the Esmeralda back to Valparaiso. He was much flattered and
caressed; but/he was treated very shabbily indeed: his men were not
paid; they were denied their prize-money from various sources; and upon
some pretext his ship was threatened with impoundment. Yet Though
Jack sometimes behaved like a simpleton by land, ~~and~~ though he
was often swindled ashore, he was sea-wise, and having provisioned
and stored his ship with *the basic supplies* everything needed to carry her *at least to* ~~beyond~~. he
handed the Chileans an ultimatum; either his men must have their
due by a given date or he should sail away. They were not
paid, and he did sail away. Yet although the Surprise's
voyage had something of the appearance of a failure, in fact the
Spanish hold on South America was broken: and although this
had not been the Admiralty's direct orders, the result gave immense
pleasure in the ~~right~~ *proper* quarters.

Furthermore Jack had aboard a singularly amiable *and gifted* young man,
the unacknowledged but much beloved illegitimate son of Prince
William. Admiral the Duke of Clarence, a zealous sailor and almost
certain to be King after his brother's death. Clarence had a
great respect for Captain Aubrey (some of Jack's actions were indeed

independent

later

some port in the kingdom or Brazil where he could complete

satisfaction

extraordinarily brilliant), and through Dr Maturin, who had treated His Highness for a variety of disease, mostly discreditable, had begged Jack to take the youth on this voyage: and young Hanson had distinguished himself as much as any loving naval father could have wished, cutting the *Esmeralda's* cable and carrying her out under fire. Yet even this was not all: on the Pacific coast Jack and Stephen had met with a small stout vessel filled with fellow members of the Royal Society, two of whom, ornithologists, were determined to cross the narrow isthmus of Panama and return to London by the Atlantic. And these excellent creatures agreed to take Jack's dispatches – the news of his famous victory and the preservation of Chile – back to the Admiralty, then in the process of forming a South African squadron. Maturin and his chief, the head of Naval Intelligence, had long since established a system of rapid communication across the Andes, and it was thanks to this arrangement that Jack received the Admiralty's beautiful reply, a signal requiring him 'to proceed to the River Plate, there to go aboard HMS *Suffolk* taking command of her and hoisting his flag, blue at the mizzen,' that had spread such happiness throughout the ship.

Yet although the ephemeral Chilean ministry had fallen, to be replaced by one of its many rivals, the satisfaction that might have been supposed to accompany an assured independence was by no means general: there were many Chileans who regretted their old friends and their declared policies. Furthermore the feeling was not confined to Chile: there were many Chilean refugees and many of their Argentinian friends who had resented the Englishmen's presence and who now even more bitterly resented their absence – to say nothing of those many, many Argentinians who so clearly remembered the British capture of Buenos Aires and the even greater number of those who looked upon them as heretics, given to cursing the Holy Father almost every day.

Both Maturin and Jacob had caught wind of this feeling both in Chile and during their very beautiful passage of the Strait; and in the afternoon

extraordinarily brilliant), and through Dr Maturin, who had treated His
Highness for a variety of diseases, mostly discreditable, had begged Jack
to take the boy on this voyage: and young Haness had distinguished
himself as much as any loving naval father could have wished, cu
cutting the <u>Esmeralda</u>'s cable and carrying her out under fire.

Yet even this was not all: on the Pacific coast Jack and Stephen had
met with a small stout vessel filled with fellow members of the Royal
Society, two of whom, ornithologists, were determined to cross the
narrow isthmus of Panama and return to London by the Atlantic.
And these excellent creatures had agreed to take Jack's dispatches — the
news of his famous victory and the preservation of Chile — back to the
Admiralty, then in the process of forming a South African squadron.
Maturin and his chief, the head of Naval Intelligence, had long
since established a system of rapid communication across the Andes.
and it was thanks to this arrangement that Jack had received the beautiful
signal requiring him 'to proceed to the River Plate, there to go
aboard HMS Suffolk, taking command of her and hoisting his flag, &c
at the mizzen' that had spread such happiness throughout the ship

Chilean
Yet though the ephemeral ministry had fallen, to be replaced by
some one of their many rivals, the satisfaction had by no mean
general: there were many who regretted their old friends and their
declared policies. Furthermore this feeling was not confined to Chile:
there were many Chilean refugees and many of their Argentinian
friends who had resented the Englishman's presence and who now even
more bitterly resented their absence — Argentinian To say nothing of
those many many Argentinians who so clearly remembered the British
capture of Buenos Aires and the even greater number of those who
looked upon them as vile heretics, given to cursing the Holy Father
almost every day.

Both Maturin and Jacob had caught word of this feeling in Chile
during their very beautiful passage of the Straits and the evening
afternoon

before they were to put in to San Pedro, a small sealing and fishing port at the bottom of an inlet on the northern shore with some sheltered arable land behind it famous for potatoes and cabbages on the one hand and prodigious mussels and crayfish on the other, Stephen said, 'My dear Jack, in the backwoods of America they say that an evil reputation is like an inextinguishable debt; and we have been so maligned on the Pacific coast that it might be prudent to arm the boats, or even to hale the ship so close to the strand that your great guns command the whole settlement.'

In the event the few inhabitants of San Pedro did not offer to challenge a reasonably powerful man-of-war moored broadside-on before their settlement, nor the powerful, cutlass-bearing seamen who walked along the quay. Yet although most of the citizens were at least partly Tierra del Fuegians and although none of them could have had any first-hand knowledge of recent events they were sullen and unfriendly, yielding only a few indifferent potatoes and wilted cabbages at an exorbitant price. However, the ship did top up her water from a clear free-running stream, no great distance from its parent glacier; and still with this blessed westerly breeze she pursued her long twisting course through the strait, Jack, Hanson and Daniel perpetually taking bearings, soundings, views of the shore (icy to the southwards, often raining to the north) and establishing a truly remarkable chart.

Stephen, who had no abilities whatsoever in this direction, confined himself to his medical duties of course (slight though they were, with a healthy crew and such an able assistant as Jacob), to watching and sometimes dissecting the birds, mammals and marine plants and creatures of the strait, and much of this he added to his letter to Christine, she being the only woman of his acquaintance who knew the difference between a jackass penguin and a macaroni and who delighted in the knowledge. She would also delight in the knowledge, reflected her lover, that these most inhospitable shores, often snowy on the south of the strait, always icy on the northern height, nevertheless sheltered at least one parrot or parakeet, a green bird with a fine red tail that flew in noisy groups in the beech-woods, and a minute humming-bird that could be seen sipping nectar from the fuchsias in Tierra del Fuego when the ship was on that side of the channel.

before they were to put in to San Pedro. a small scaly and fishy port ~~on the west~~ at the bottom of an inlet on the northern shore with some sheltered arable land behind it famous for potatoes and cabbages on the one hand and prodigious mussels and crayfish on the other. Stephen said 'My dear Jack, in the backwoods of America they say that an evil reputation is like an inextinguishable debt; and we have been so maligned on the Pacific coast that you might think it prudent to arm the boats, or even to hale the ship so close to the strand that your great guns command the ~~entire~~ *whole* settlement.'

In the event the few inhabitants of San Pedro did not choose to ~~take~~ challenge a powerful man-of-war moored broadside-on before their settlement, nor the ~~cutlass bea~~ powerful, cutlass-bearing seamen who walked about along the quay. But although most of them were at least partially Terra del Fuegian and although none of them could have had any first-hand knowledge of recent events they were sullen and unfriendly, yielding only a few indifferent potatoes and no cabbages at an ~~ever~~ exorbitant ~~por~~ price. However the ship did top up her water from a clear, free-running stream, and still with this blessed westerly breeze she pursued her long, thirsty course through the strait. Jack, Hanson and Daniel perpetually taking bearings, soundings, views of the shore (icy to the southward, often raining to the north) and establishing a truly remarkable chart.

Stephen, who had no abilities whatsoever in this direction, confined himself to his medical duties of course (slight they were, with a healthy crew and such an able assistant as Jacob), to watching and sometimes dissecting the birds, mammals, and marine plants and creatures of the ~~shores~~ of the strait, and much of this he added to his letter to Christine, she being the only woman of his acquaintance who knew the difference between a Jackass penguin and a macaroni and who thoroughly delighted in the knowledge.

here I must have a reasonably comprehensive account of the Strait's natural history. It to be gathered from [Hoffki?] book, Darwin, & Enc. Brit
the parrots can appear in number (+ other exotics? humming birds) in a sheltering wind from the NW (or wherever) It could extend to 200 words ? often

He was reasonably well engaged with this letter one afternoon after dinner when Jack, abandoning his fiddle, returned to his surveying, and Stephen, cloging his passage on Port Egmont hens (often to be seen), lifted his head to Hanson's reiterated 'Sir, if you please.'

'Why, Master dear' – for Horatio Hanson was acting-master of the ship – 'I fear you have been waiting. I never heard you.'

'Not at all, sir: it was only that Dr Jacob feared you might have overlooked your appointment.' At this moment a tiny chime could be heard in the bosom of both, for each possessed wonderfully accurate repeating watches, the one a replacement of the minute timepiece that Stephen had given to Christine, the other Prince William's parting gift to his son. 'God love us all, and may I be forgiven,' cried Stephen, leaping up. 'It is half three – I am late.'

'Mind your step, sir,' said Hanson, steadying him. 'It is blowing up uncommon stiff from the west-north-west – has veered three points in half an hour, and *Ringle* is reefing hard.'

They made their way forward to the fairly well-lit and now vacant space in the sickberth which the surgeons reserved for anatomizing – for the past few days they had been busy on a singular, probably undescribed dolphin; and as they carefully pared away, separated and described the muscular parts so they gave them to the cook's mates, standing there with buckets. The bones they kept for themselves. But today they had been obliged to stop. The frigate's motion was too great, and in spite of their skill and care their cutting was by no means accurate with the deck so very much awash.

'We are making ready to lie to, sir,' said Hanson in his ear. 'And the Captain says he will pass the word when it is fit for you to come on deck. In the mean time he desires you and Dr Jacob will stand by to deal with casualties.'

The first, to his own infinite shame, was Harding, the senior lieutenant – a straightforward fibula and tibia, which they very soon splinted and

He was reasonably well engaged with this letter one afternoon after dinner when Jack, abandoning his fiddle, returned to his surgery, and Stephen, closing his passage on Port Egmont hens, lifted his head to Hanson's reiterated 'Sir. If you please.'

'Why, Master Rear?' — for Horatio Hanson was acting master of the day — 'I fear you have been waiting. I never heard you.'

'Not at all, sir: it was only that Jacob feared you might have overlooked your appointment.' At this moment a tiny chime could be heard in the bosom of each, for both possessed of wonderfully accurate repeating watches, the one given to Stephen by his grandfather, the other to Hanson by Prince William. 'God love us all and may I be forgiven.' cried Stephen leaping up. 'It is half three — I am late.'

'Mind your step, sir,' said Hanson, steadying him. 'It is blowing up uncommon stiff still from the WNW — has veered three points in half an hour, and Ringle is reefing hard.'

They made their way forward to the fairly well-lit and now vacant space in the sickberth which the surgeons reserved for anatomizing — they were busy on a singular, probably undescribed small dolphin and as they carefully pared away. separated and described the muscular parts so they gave them to the cook's mates, standing here with buckets. The bones they kept for themselves. But presently they were obliged to stop. The ship's motion was too great; and in spite of all their skill and care, the deck was awash — their cutting by no means accurate.

'We are making ready to lie to, sir.' said Hanson in his ear. 'And the Captain says he will pass the word when it is fit for you to come on deck. In the mean time he desires you with this and so Jacob will stand by to deal with casualties.'

The first. to his infinite shame. was Harding. the first lieutenant — a straightforward brazen febula and tibia. which they very soon splinted and

febia o

bound up: then came the usual series of bumps and bruises, diminishing as the furious gust blew itself out and ending with the Captain's compliments brought by Awkward Davies, and if now they chose to come on deck they would see 'a sight like a madhouse's washing-day – God love us – what rigging we have is fair stuffed, *stuffed*, with fucking poll-parrots and God knows what. Which I am to bring you up and cop three hundred lashes if you fall.'

Stephen had of course heard of the South American parrots and he had often seen their little troops, but only from a distance, identifiable from their manner of flight and from their brilliant colour, so very unlike the general drabness of the Strait; and so eager was he to reach the first, entangled in the leeward shrouds, that he would certainly have gone over the side but for Davies' powerful restraining hand. And it was not only parakeets, though they of course were the most obvious and the most eagerly coveted by hands, who were perfectly accustomed to the African race: even more spectacular and even more wounding were the many kinds of minute birds, including Stephen's Tierra del Fuegian honey-sucker, that had been dashed against the rigging or the remaining sails with such force that in spite of their lightness they were quite shattered and as the blast died away, deck, lighter rigging and scuppers were jewelled all over with their pitiful but still brilliant fragments. Some of the more solid birds, particularly the parakeets and some red-crested woodpeckers, could be revived and patched to some degree, but upon the whole it was a most dispiriting task, the more so since there was very little hope of identification in most cases. Still Stephen, seconded by his mate, did what they could in the way of retrieval, mostly of skins (exceptionally difficult on that scale) and tiny bones: they took quantities of notes and they did a little something to increase their knowledge of this almost untouched avifauna.

For two and even three days after that furious blast the waters of the Strait remained strikingly turbulent, particularly in the Narrows, and great beds of kelp, torn loose from their basis, floated on every hand, sometimes endangering the rudder, sometimes checking the ship's way, and always disturbing birds, cetaceans and ordinary level-headed fishes. Nevertheless in spite of kelp, unexpected currents and strange vagaries of tide off a number of headlands, the ship's whole passage of the Strait, before she turned north, well out in the full Atlantic, with the Cape of the Eleven Thousand Virgins broad on larboard bow, lasted only three hours more than nine days.

'We are making pretty good time,' said Jack, 'and I think we may look into Port Desire and Bahia Blanca without keeping the Admiral waiting. He was not to sail till the twelfth.'

'Would you ever tell me, has he a numerous fleet?'

'Pretty considerable: three squadrons, of which ours, the blue, is of course the smallest – but, Stephen, do not think for a moment that I complain. Of course it is **the** smallest, being blue. But had it been half the size, I should still have given my **right** hand for it. Good Lord above: a flag at last! It was amazingly kind of them. Do not think for a moment that I complain, dear Stephen.'

'It had not occurred to me at all, at all,' said Stephen. And

bound up: then came the usual series of bumps and thumps, dimminishly as the furious gust blew itself out and ending with the captain's compliment brought by Awkward Davies. and if now he chose to come on deck he would a sight like a madhouse's washing-day - God love us - what rigging we have fair slitted, slitted, with freeing parrots and God knows what, in which I am to bring you and cop 300 lashes if you fall.'

Long, long had Stephen heard of the little parrots of the South America forest, but he had never seen one and nor he would fairly have leapt on deck but for Davies' powerful restraining hand

more. perhaps 200 words, when more I know

For two and even three days after that furious blast the waters of the Strait remained stirring, turbulent, particularly in the narrows. and great beds of kelp, apparently torn loose floated on every hand. sometime endangering the rudder. sometime checking their/ and always disturbing birds. cetaceans. and ordinary level-headed fishes Nevertheless their whole passage before they turned north. well out in the full Atlantic. took them only three hours. more than nine days.

'We are making pretty good time.' said Jack. 'and I think we may look into Port Desire and Bahia Blanca without keep the Admiral waiting. He was not to be said till the Twelfth.'

'Would you ever tell me. has he a numerous fleet?.'

'Pretty considerable: three squadrons. of which ours. the blue, is of course. the smallest — but Stephen. do not think for a moment that I complain. Of course it is the smallest. being blue. But were it one half the size I should have given my right hand for it. Good Lord above: a flag at last! It was amazingly kind of them. Do not think for a moment that I complain. dear Stephen.'

'It had not occurred to me at all, at all.' said Stephen. And

he went on, 'Since my ill-bred questioning is so prosperous – and to be sure it is very ill-bred indeed – may I ask why you mean to stop at these South American ports, when I understood you to say we could sail home with what was in the hold?'

'Why, for fresh water and meat, of course, to say nothing of vegetables and fruit. We could probably have got home, of course, but verminous, half-starved and rotten with scurvy: but that would have been a desperate stroke, in a God-damned desperate situation, one that a man could not stand. But now the case is altered. I am to join Lord Leyton in the River Plate, and I make no doubt – for he is a very active officer, as I know full well – that he will take the fleet down and across to the Cape with the utmost dispatch, and I prefer to be ready to weigh at the first hint of a signal, with the last cask of biscuit aboard and a well-fed, active, healthy crew – no shore-leave will be allowed.'

'But, my dear, *Surprise* is to go home, as you very well know, with your dispatches and all our letters home; and once there she reverts to the station of a private ship. Ever since we left Magellan's Strait and steered north the people have become increasingly aware of this, and the joy that filled the *Surprise* has sensibly diminished day by day. You know how unhappy our men from Shelmerston were when they were paid off with the peace and how wonderfully they revived when you took them aboard.'

'Certainly I know it very well, and I am going to use all what influence I may have to ease her back into the service. The squadron is pitifully short of frigates, and since I understand that our duty down there is the protection of the Indian and Chinese trade, nothing could be more useful than a nimble weatherly ship like *Surprise*. And I beg you will do the same. But even if we cannot succeed directly, I am allowed my bargemen and a good many other followers – I have little doubt that I shall house a score or so of the rest among my friends. And for those that are left, if there *are* any left, merchant shipping has revived wonderfully, and a seaman with a good character from the Royal Navy will not wait long for a berth.'

JUST AS IT HAD BEEN Hanson who first sighted Cape Pilar on their eastward leg, at the very opening of the Strait, so it was his particular friend Daniel who, spending his watch below in the foretopgallant crosstrees, caught the leading-mark for Port Desire in his glass, checked it twice, and called,

9

he went on. 'Since my ill-bred questioning is so prosperous — and to be sure it is very ill-bred indeed — may I ask why you mean to stop at the South America ports?, when I understood you to say we could sail home with what was in the hold?'.

'Why, for fresh water and fresh meat, of course; to say nothing of vegetables and fruit. We could probably have got home, of course, but retmuchose, half-starved and rotten with scurvy: but that was a desperate stroke in a God-damned desperate situation, one that a man could not stand. But now the case is altered. I am to join Lord Leyton in the River Plate, and I make no doubt — for he is a very active officer, as I know full well — that he will take us down and across to the Cape with the utmost despatch, and I prefer to be ready to weigh at the first heave of a signal, with the last cask of bread biscuit aboard and a well-fed active crew — no shore-leave will be allowed.'

'But, my dear, Surprise is to go home, as you very well know, with your despatches and all our letters home; and once there she reverts to the station of a private ship. Ever since we left off Magellan Strait the people and slewed north the people have become increasingly aware of this, and the frigate has sensibly deteriorated day by day You know how unhappy our men from Shelmerston were when they were paid off with the peace and how wonderfully they revived when you took them aboard.'

'Certainly I know it very well, and I am going to use all what interest I may have to have her back in the service. The squadron is pitifully short of frigates, and sure I understand that our duty down there is the protection of the Brazilian and Chinese trade, nothing could be more useful than a weatherly ship like Surprise. And I beg you will do the same. But even if we cannot succeed directly, I am allowed my bargemen and a good many others — I have little doubt that I shall house a score or so of the rest among my friend. And for those that are left, I may are a good character from the Royal Navy will not want long for a berth

Just as it had been Hanson who first sighted Cape Pilar on their eastward leg, at the very opening of the strait, so it was his particular friend Daniel who, splicing his watch below in the fore/topsail crosstrees, caught the leading-mark for Port Desire in his glass, checked it twice and called

'On deck, there. On deck: St Paul's Rock, twelve to fifteen miles on the larboard bow. Dim. Comes and goes.'

It came and went because of a heavy sea inshore that covered it entirely from time to time, if not with green water then with foam; and although the rollers moderated somewhat inshore, the frigate had an uneasy time, mooring in the sullen turbulences this side of the primitive mole-dirty water from some untimely flash-flood.

'I once saw a rhea here, some way inland,' observed Stephen, as he and Jacob were walking along the mean street (obscurely strewn with drowned dogs) to speak to the port-captain about water and vegetables. 'The South American ostrich, somewhat smaller than the African bird – a most inferior creature.'

'Ah?' said Jacob: and then 'I believe this must be the captain's house.'

The port-captain half rose when they came in, but he was far from cordial and he said that he could not recommend the town water after this diabolic flood and all the nastiness it brought.

Stephen spoke about the country inland, a hacienda he had visited, the kindness of the people. He and the others were of course speaking Spanish and after a while the port-captain said that there happened to be a clean spring at no great distance, but they would have to pay the proprietor a fee. 'It is not for myself, you understand. For my own part I am astonishingly generous, generous to a fault, even lavish . . .' He spoke of his faults at some length and then, having called for coffee, he asked in a confidential, almost affectionate tone, 'Why they, obviously old and rancid Christians, consorted with those vile heretics?' And when Stephen made the usual gesture of extreme poverty, rubbing thumb over knuckle, the captain shook his head, saying 'Ah, when the Devil drives . . . I shall send my boy with your men to Anita's spring, but they must be very respectful to her, and pluck off their hats. Her sister, Helena, the werewolf, will provide cabbages.'

So she did, fine upstanding plants, but without the least appearance of pleasure or (perhaps understandably) of common humanity: and both in these transactions and in a few others along the edge of the market the Surprises noticed a sullenness, a strong inclination to stare, muttering; while after some of their transactions the sellers could be seen to wash the coins or rub them industriously in the grit underfoot.

'On deck there. On deck: St Paul's rock twelve to fifteen miles on the larboard bow. Dim. Comes & goes.'

It came and went because of a heavy sea inshore that covered in enlivened from time to time. Y not with green water then with foam; and although it moderated somewhat inshore, the frigate had an uneasy time of it, mooring in the sullen turbulence this side of the primitive mole — dirty water from some untimely flash-flood.

'I once saw a thea here, some way inland,' observed Stephen, as he and Jacob were walking along the main street (obscurely strewn with drowned dogs) to speak to the port-captain about water and vegetables. 'Indeed? So √

American tech, something to tun in Africa, most impressive of 'Ah?' and 'I believe ten in captain's hen

He half rose when they came in, but he was far from cordial and he said that he would not recommend the town water after this utter diabolic flood and all the nastiness it brought.'

Stephen spoke about the country inland, a hacienda he had visited, the kindness of the people. He and the others were of course speaking Spanish and after a while the port-captain said that there happened to be a clear spring at no great distance, but they would have to pay the proprietor a fee. 'It is not for myself, you understand — I am astonishingly generous, generous to a fault, even lavish...' He spoke of his family at some length and then, having called for coffee, he asked in a confidential, almost affectionate tone. 'Are they obviously old and rancid Christians, consorted with their vile heretics?' And when Stephen made the usual gestures of extreme perplexity, rubbing his climb over knuckle, the captain shook his head, saying 'Ah, when the Devil drives... I shall send my boy with the men to Anita's spring, but they too must be very respectful to her and pluck off their hats. Her sister Helena, who is a werewolf, will provide the cabbages.'

So she did, fine upstanding plants, but without the least appearance of pleasure or (perhaps understandably) of common humanity, and both in their transaction and in a favoured along the edge of the market noticed a sullenness, a strong inclination stare, muttering; while after some of these transactions the sellers could be seen to wash the coins or rub them industriously on the pavement. got under foot.

Even if the *Surprise*, with her singularly fine lines and her thirty-six-gun frigate's towering mainmast, had not been so recognizable to a sailor's eye, her ensign would have identified her almost anywhere in the world, for on reverting to her function as a surveying-vessel under Admiralty command she had also reverted to the white ensign. At Bahia Blanca, their next port of call, Stephen, who was the natural emissary on such occasions, reported the same sullen apathy, no unmingled with a reluctance to sell, exorbitant prices and injurious expressions.

'Brother, you are playing at least half a tone too high,' said Jack that evening as they sawed away after an early supper.

'Am I?' cried Stephen, looking attentively at his fingers and twanging the string. 'So I am. I do beg your pardon. It is the shrill bitterness of my soul that makes its way out, I fear.'

'I am so sorry to impose these odious duties upon you, Stephen – pray take a sup of port – but you know, of course you know only too well, that when you and all your people have been without long enough you will descend to the basest means to relieve your wants.'

'I am not sure that the response is altogether civil: but be that as it may, I will tell you, Jack, that if they are bad in Port Desire and worse in Bahia, they are likely to be downright outrageous in the River Plate, where we are to meet the South African ships. Yet if I am not mistaken we are likely to be there well before Lord Leyton – well before even your little squadron . . .'

'What the Devil do you mean by *my little squadron*? It is a perfectly normal squadron, rather large than otherwise. Two ships of the line apart from *Suffolk*: a fifty-gun ship, two considerable sloops of war . . .'

'Hush, hush, Jack. Never fly into a passion, soul,' cried Stephen, seeing that his friend was seriously annoyed. 'Sure you must know after all this time that we use *little* as an endearment – a meliorative term, as one says my *little Puss* to a handsome Amazon that weighs fifteen stone in her

Even if the *Surprise*, with her singularly fine lines and her 36-gun frigate's towering mainmast had not been so recognizable to a sailor's eye, her ensign would have identified her almost anywhere in the world, for on reverting to her function as a surveying-vessel under Admiralty command she had also reverted to the white ensign. At Bahia Blanco, their next port of call, Stephen, who was the natural emissary on such occasions, reported the same sullen antipathy, not unmingled with a reluctance to sell, exorbitant prices, and injurious expressions.

'Brother, you are playing at least a half-tone too high,' said Jack that evening as they sawed away after an early supper.

'Am I?' cried Stephen, looking attentively at his fingers & twanging his strings. 'So I am. I do beg your pardon. It is the sheer bitterness of my soul that makes it sway out, I fear.'

'I am so sorry to impose these odious duties upon you, Stephen — pray take a sup of port — but you know, of course you know only too well, that when you and all, yeret people, have been without long enough you will descend to the basest means to relieve them.'

'I am not sure that that is altogether civil; but be that as it may, I will tell you, Jack, that if they are bad in Port Desire and worse in Bahia, they are likely to be downright outrageous in the River Plate. For if I understood you aright, we are to meet the South African ships right up against the city. Yet if I am not mistaken we are likely to be there well before Lord Leyla — well before even your little squadron ...'

'What the Devil do you mean my little squadron? It is a perfectly normal squadron, & rather large than otherwise. Two ships of the line apart from Suffolk, a fifty-gun ship. We consider the ships of war ...'

'Hush, hush, Jack. Never fly ink & passion, soul,' said Stephen, seeing that his friend was quite seriously annoyed. 'Sure you must know after all this time that we use little as an endearment — a meliorative term, as one says my little purse to a handsome Amazon that weighs fifteen stone in her

shift. So we arrive, do you follow me now, well before his lordship, whom God preserve, and our natural allies, all because of our commendable zeal. Now let me beg you, for all love, to moor your ship close in against the southern shore for so much as an egg, an egg: for in a considerable city fanaticism can swell to a most surprising and horrible extent.'

At the end of the particularly grave adagio Jack put down his bow and said, 'Should you dislike it very much if we were to leave Bahia out of our plans? Our water and the cabbages have held out uncommon well and I had as soon push on quietly, if you understand me, to the River Plate, where there is a great resort of merchantmen and all sort of people that supply their needs, chandlers, smiths and the like: you are not dependent on the local werewolf. Not that I have anything to say against werewolves: the gentlewoman was perfectly civil, and her cabbages have stood up admirably.'

'I should not dislike it at all. Bahia has by all accounts some tolerable strands, but nothing in the way of lakes or marshland within striking distance: Jacob and I have an immense amount of sorting, reconstituting, classifying and preserving to do, and I had as soon sail on northwards – quietly, as you put it so well, quietly putting our collections in order.'

Quietly indeed they sailed along, with gentle breezes that wafted them generally northwards at something in the nature of five miles in the hour, northwards to even warmer seas. Little activity was called for, apart from the nice adjustment of the sails, and although the exact routine of the ship was never relaxed nor her very strict rules of cleanliness, these long sunny days with a soldier's wind seemed to many the ideal of a seaman's life – regular, steady, traditional meals with the exact allowance of grog; hornpipes in the last dogwatch, the deep melody of the Doctor's 'cello from the cabin and the cheerful sound of the gunroom's dinner; the future lost in a haze somewhere north of the equator.

So the golden days went by, and Stephen's mound of tiny skins mounted up, very carefully dried and treated against mites, against the voracious

ship. So we arrive, do you follow me, now?, well before her lordship, whom God preserve, and our natural allies, all because of our commendable zeal. Now let me beg you, for all love, to moor your ship close in against the southern shore, and restrain to come as it were among the sheltering trees, and never to send ashore for so much as an egg, an egg: for in a considerable city fanaticism and resentment can swell to a most surprising and horrible extent.

At the end of this particularly grave allegro, Jack put down his tea and said 'Should you dislike it very much if we were to leave Bahia out of our plans? Our water, and the cabbages have held out uncommon well and I had as soon push on quiet, if you understand me, to the River Plate, where there is a great resort of merchantmen and all sorts of people that supply their wants, chandlers and the like: you are not dependent on the local werewolf. Not that I have anything to say against werewolves: the gentlewomen were perfectly civil, and her cabbage have stood up admirably.'

'I should not mind it at all. Bahia has, by all accounts some tolerable strands, but nothing in the way of lakes or marshland with stinking mitano: I had Jacob & I have an immense amount of sorting, classifying and preserving to do, and I had as soon sail on northward - quietly, as you put it so well, to quietly pulling our collection in order.

Quietly indeed they sailed along, with gentle breezes that wafted them & generally northwards to ever warmer seas. Little activity was called for, apart from the nice adjustment of the sails, and although the exact routine of the ship was never relaxed nor her strict rules of cleanliness, these long sunny days with a soldier's wind seemed to many the ideal of a seaman's life. — regular, steady, traditional meals with the exact allowance of grog; hornpipes in the last dog-watch, the deep melody of the Captain's cello from the cabin and the cheerful sound of the gunroom's dinner. The future lost in the haze somewhere north of the equator.

So these golden days went by, and Stephen's mound of tiny skins mounted up, very carefully dried and treated against moth, the voracious

cockroaches that no amount of sulphurous fumigation could eliminate from the ultimate depths of the hold, their survivors breeding with extraordinary rapidity.

By the time they were in flying-fish water again, the *Surprise* and her people had settled down to this very agreeable form of life – some few cases of sunburn and alleged moon-pall by night, to occupy Poll Skeeping and Maggie, and a series of quite deep, painful wounds or rather hook-billed bites from those parakeets that did not choose to be tamed; but for once, for *once*, no steady dosing for the pox. With a perfectly competent, conscientious, but by no means tyrannical first lieutenant, Jack Aubrey and his clerk could devote their hours to gathering all the scattered surveying material from the various notebooks and journals and cast it into the regular form most valued by the Hydrographical Department. They were quite near the end of their work on the immense south Pacific crescent, at the northern tip of the Chonos Archipelago, which Jack had surveyed in freezing drizzle with a team of zealous and remarkably amiable young Chilean officer-cadets when the expected news came below. With the Master's duty, Mr Wells begged to tell Captain Aubrey that the leading-marks for the River Plate were clear from the masthead, almost due north-north-west.

They were clearer still by the last dogwatch, when the declining sun lit them from behind; and in the morning the *Surprise* was well into the whole vast bay. All day long, with a gently favouring breeze they sailed up it until both shores could clearly be seen, and a fair amount of shipping: but never a sign of a man-of-war.

Farther, farther, with no more than her foretopsail now: a pause for dinner; and drinking his coffee on deck afterwards Jack said to Stephen, 'May I ask you and Dr Jacob to run up to the island with Wantage and make sure that our salute will be returned? This reception is so very curious that I should like to make quite certain. Mr Harding, please be so good as to have the blue cutter put over the side.'

The island was the chief of the many administrative centres: it was from the battery high on the seaward cliff that salutes were answered; and usually the place was like a fairly busy hive, with customs, quarantine and harbour-dues officials swarming all over it, together with soldiers, sailors, marines and those grave gentlemen in long black coats, black-scabbarded swords, black neckcloths and black wigs who were said to be very high in the administration. At present the place was singularly quiet, almost motionless, and since a salute was rarely returned without a good deal of bustle, the silence made all hands uneasy. It was known throughout the service that an unreturned salute was practically a casus belli. In any event it was the gravest insult and one that put an end to all communication with the shore. And to fire a salute without assurance that it would be returned was strictly forbidden. The question did not often arise, but in this case the atmosphere was so uncommon that Jack did not intend to run the risk.

Yet while the coxswain was summoning his boat's crew Harding

cockroaches that lurked in the ultimate recesses of the hold. their
survivors breeding with extraordinary rapidity

By the time they were in flying-fish water again, the Surprise
and her people had settled down to this very agreeable form of
life — some few cases of sunburn (or moon-pall by night) to
occupy Poll Skeeping and Maggie, and a series of quite deep,
painful wounds or rather hook-billed bites from those parakeets that
did not choose to be tamed, but for once, for once no steady
dosing for the pox. With a perfectly competent, conscientious
by no means tyrannical first lieutenant Jack Aubrey and his
clerk could devote their hours to gathering all the scattered survey
material from its notebooks and journals and cast it in the regular
form most valued by the Hydrographical Department. They were
quite near the end of their immense immense extent, at the northern
lip of the Chonos Archipelago, surveyed with a team of zealous
and remarkably amiable young Chilean officer-cadets when the
expected news came below. With the master's duty, Mr Wells
begged to tell the Captain Aubrey that the leading-marks for the
River Plate were clear from the masthead

They were clearer still by the last dog-watch, when the declining
sun lit them from behind; and in the morning they were well
into the whole vast bay. All day, with a favouring breeze,
they sealed up it until both shores could be seen and a fair
amount of shipping: but never a sign of a man-of-war.

Farther, farther, with no more than topsails now: a pause
for dinner; and drinking coffee on deck afterwards Jack said to
Stephen 'May I ask you and Dr Jacob to run up to the island
with Wantage and make sure that our salute will be returned? This
is so curious a reception that I should like to make certain. And
Mr Harding, please to so good as to the blue cutter over
the side.'

But while the coxswain was summoning the cutter's crew Harding
yet

said to Jack, 'Forgive me, sir, but I believe I see a craft clearing from the lee-side. Yes, sir,' lowering his glass, 'I think it is one of their medicoes and a couple of dirty mates.' He peered again. 'Yes: a dirty, ill-looking crew in a dirty, ill-looking craft.'

They did not improve on closer acquaintance: at fifty yards from the frigate's side a man stood up and bawled 'Quarantine.'

Harding had a ladder put over and the party's leader, wearing a black coat and a yellow wig, followed by a youth with an ink-horn, came aboard quite nimbly. 'Dr Quental,' said the man in a very loud voice. 'Health. Speak Portuguese?' Wantage, who was fluent in the language, made as though to answer, but Stephen checked him. 'I am the surgeon of this ship, sir,' he said in Latin. 'Dr Maturin, at your service. I do not have the pleasure of speaking Portuguese, but I should be happy to answer any questions you choose to ask in Latin. And so will my colleague, Dr Jacob.'

Dr Quental put as good a face on it as he could, and with more ease than the company expected he repeated a list of disorders by class: '*Exanthematici? Critici? Phlogistici? Dolorosi? Quietales? Motorii? Suppressorii? Evacuatorii? Deformes? Vitia?*'

Stephen considered all these, one by one, shaking his head after due reflection and then inviting their guest to come and view what invalids the ship possessed.

Poll Skeeping and Maggie had had plenty of time: their few patients (all with mill strains or broken bones apart from one with raging toothache, to be dealt with tomorrow, when his particular friend the armourer had finished a powerful pair of forceps to his own satisfaction) were correctly rigid in their cots, washed pink, brushed and incapable of movement, almost of drawing breath, so tight-strained were the sheets. Dr Quental was much impressed, much gratified by a draught of rum, happy to accept the compliment of a neatly-cased French amputating saw, and perfectly willing to give *Surprise* a clean bill of health. He also stated that in his considered opinion the fort would not hesitate to answer the ship's salute with exactly the same number of guns; having sorted his Latin with some care while he finished his glass, he told Stephen that he was an anti-clerical, that he had nothing to do

said to Jack. 'Forgive me, sir, but I believe I see a craft & cleary from the lee-side. Yes, sir.' lowering his glass. 'I think it is one of their medicoes and a couple of dirty mates.' He peered again 'Ya a dirty, ill-looking & crew in a dirty ill-looking craft.'

They did not improve on closer acquaintance: at fifty yards from Frigate's side a man stood up and bawled 'Quarantine.'

Hardly had a ladder put over and the leading man, in a black coat and a yellow wig followed by a youth with an ink-horn came aboard quite nimbly. 'Dr Quental,' he said very loud. Health. Speak Portuguese?.' Wantage who was fluent in a language made as if to answer but Stephen checked him. 'I am the surgeon of this ship,' he said 'Dr Maturin, at your service. I do not have the pleasure of speaking Portuguese but I should be happy to converse answer any question you choose to ask, in Latin.'

Dr Quental put a reasonably good face on he could and if not with more of ease than the company expected he & repeated a list of classes of disorders — exanthematici, critici, phlogistici, dolorosi mentales, quietales, motorii, suppressorii, evacuatorii deformes, vitia, to which Stephen gently all of which Stephen gravely consented, shaking his head at each instance and then inviting their & quental to come below and view what invalids the ship possessed. Poll Skeeping and Maggie had had plenty of time; their few patient (all mild strains, broken bones & one toothache, to be dealt with tomorrow, when the armoured stores have fall fashioned suitably massive forceps) were suitably cleaned an rigid in their cots washed. brushed and incapable of movement. almost of drawing breath. Dr Quental was suitably impressed, suitably gratified by a draught of rum, happy to accept the gift of a neat, cased French amputating saw. and perfectly willing to give Surgeon a clean bill of health. On being told also stated in his considered opinion that the fort would not hesitate to answer the ship's salute. and, having settled his Latin with some ease, he told Stephen that he was an anti-clerical, that he had nothing to say

with the public burning of heretics, and that he dared say there were very good men everywhere: among Jews, for example, or blacks, or even worse.

[The manuscript breaks off here for several pages—see O'Brian's note, opposite page—and the narrative is continued in the typsescript.]

for example . or blacks, or even

(1)

to religious intolerance and that he dared say that there were very good men everywhere . even among Jews / or worse.

the MS p 17 follows the typed MS / TS follows

a typed p 15 & 16

from this point I continued with the typewriter : I have change back to this again

pp 15 & 16 ch I
in TS

'Sir,' said Wantage in Stephen's ear as the Rio boat pulled away, 'his mates that did not go below with the Doctor, told me there was a rare old rumpus in the town last night, when some of people from a barque out of Boston, the Boston in the colonies, stood up at a vigil and said it was great nonsense to say you were allowed only one wife: one wife at a time. "Look at King Solomon," they said; and it was taken very much amiss. Then one of them called out that he did not give a fig for the Pope of Rome, and fighting broke out. They said five Protestant houses were set on fire, and it might be much worse tomorrow, with the arrival of the Legate.'

'What's a legate?' asked Jack, when Stephen told him of this.

'In England they were usually called nuncios,' said Stephen: but in answer to a very severe look he added; 'An ambassador, as you might say – often plenipotentiary.'

'Well, I hope the silly villains have got it wrong,' said Jack with a look of strong dissatisfaction. 'This is the very last moment to become religious and start looking for stakes, gunpowder and – what do you call those things?'

'Sanbenitos.'

'Just so: sanbenitos. All we want to do is to fill up our water, buy a few fresh provisions and no doubt some wholesome fruit – we do not want to be racked, scourged and burnt: we get plenty of that at sea, free, gratis and for nothing – and pay our compliment to the Governor. Oh, that *Suffolk* would come in, followed by the rest of the blue squadron, then by Lord Leyton with his ships and hey for Cape Town with never a papist in sight for the next ten thousand miles . . . I beg pardon, dear Stephen,' he added, looking earnestly into Stephen's face. 'I really did not mean to be unkind or personal.'

'I am sure you did not, my dear,' said Stephen. 'Pray when do you mean to start the salute?'

'Just as soon as the gunner tells the officer of the watch that all is right and ready, oh; and the officer of the watch tells Harding to his astonishment that we are all ready. Then, when I have begged Harding to proceed we shall, with luck, hear that fine measured boom, boom, boom. Twelve guns is usual for Rio, and I know that Harding is having the irons heated; for, do you see, with a red-hot iron in your touch-hole you cannot miss fire and have one of those embarrassing pauses in the solemn round. He is as eager as I am to have the barky as trim as the Royal yacht on occasions like this.

The day itself was by no means as trim as it would have been, but for the Legate's visitation; yet even so, at tea-time Killick, came in, followed by Grimble, a procession of two, bearing the tea-tray (a great Spanish salver captured long ago) and a reasonable amount of anchovy toast, tea-cakes and a noble muffin.

Jack took tea seriously, as well he might, being so much exposed to the elements; indeed, he finished the two-men's muffin single handed; and then, wiping his buttery fingers, he directed an intelligent, almost a political look at Stephen, paused for a while, and then said, in substance, exactly what Stephen had expected him to say. 'There are, as you know better than I – far better, indeed, a good many of our people are . . .' Here he hesitated trying to find which was least offensive: Papists? Romans? Mumbo-Jumbo certainly would not do. *People of the old faith* sounded obsequious.

'Most of them are Irish, of course; though quite a few come from the English north country. And then there are the mere foreigners . . . that is to say, the foreigners.'

'There is something to be said for the word Catholics. It is in general use in Ireland.'

'Just so: thank you, Stephen. Well, in strange towns you quite often lead your band to a place where they hear what they expect to hear – a place where they are quite at home.'

'Just so. And, if you recall, I nearly always bring them back to the ship sober.'

'Indeed you do: thoughtful, contemplative and, as you say, dead sober. Now it just happened to cross my mind that was you to take them all to the cathedral, where I have no doubt the Legate will be pontificating, as is but right and proper, and if they were to be perfectly neat, fit to pass an Admiral's inspection, most uncommon solemn and pious, if you understand me, and was they to sing out good and hearty in the right places, it might tend to create a good impression, and persuade his Holiness that we were not all a band of gin-sodden raparees, given over entirely to whoredom and things I do not like even to mention. I hope you do not find my suggestion offensive, Stephen? For it is only a suggestion, to you see, not in any sense an order.'

'A very good suggestion, too. And I shall pass the word about my fellow-papists, letting them know, among other things, that it is for the honour of the ship that we should not all be blacked with a whole number of brushes – Lutherans, bigots, church-burners, destroyers of monasteries, sodomites and a number of other words that will instantly occur to your mind. But first, with your permission I will go ashore and gather what information I can: at present I swim in a sea of unknowing. The only thing that is at all clear is that upon the whole do not love us as much as they should.'

What he said was quite true. Neither the British seamen nor the Royal Navy seemed really popular. Quite early in the morning a large scow, filled with much of the city's night-soil, heaved its massy burden overboard so close to the frigate's side that her paintwork was horribly fouled and her yardarms much endangered: all this to the cry 'Filthy sods,' which the Portguese had obviously learnt from a merchant-man and which they repeated with unflagging zeal for a very long time, stopping only when some facetious hands from an incoming trawler started throwing their more putrid cargo on to *Surprise*'s deck. The trawler, curiously enough, was garlanded if not with roses, then at least with some bright pink tropical flowers. Nor was she alone in this: very considerable numbers of other fishing-craft, from whalers down to one-rod tunny-men, came swarming up the bay.

During a pause in the hoots, the pelting and the obscene gestures, Stephen and Jacob returned, unhurt, unmolested, undefiled – they did indeed look very like foreigners, poor souls. They asked Jack to come below, and in the cabin Stephen said, 'Sir, I shall speak for us both, if I may, although Dr Jacob's information is of greater value than mine and his connexions far more varied. In the very first place the extreme clerical what I might call right wing means to overthrow the governor and the government tonight or tomorrow. The Legate, who has great influence with the very large service population and above all with their leaders is here to prevent or at least to soften this movement: the ultra-clericals have little in the way of armed sup-

port, and that is one of the reasons why they have made so much of this alleged Protestant business, and why we were pelted with dung. May I say how extraordinarily wise you have been not to retaliate? To continue: this is the day upon which the fishing-boats are blessed, a very considerable feast indeed, a holiday of obligation.' He looked at his watch. 'I shall not go on prating any longer, but let me beg you to come on deck now, with your glass: and if necessary to go into the top to see the Legate arrive at the top of the steps from which he blesses the fishermen and their craft.'

Jack Aubrey did exactly what he was asked to do, giving Jacob a hand at the last stage; and there they stood all three, gazing out to starboard at the far, but not so very far, side of the harbour, where a noble flight of stairs led down to the water. At the side of the step stood soldiers in scarlet cloaks; and on the water the boat's kedges dropped, sails stowed, floated quietly for their blessing. Suddenly the prodigious, all-pervading sound of the vast crowd dropped to something not far from silence, instantly filled by the glorious sound of trumpets; and as the Legate, a fine tall upright figure in a white gown, advanced to the head of the steps, the people cheered to the very vault of the sky.

'By God, he's black,' said Jack Aubrey, and a moment later his face was contorted with emotion.

'He is very happy,' murmured Stephen. 'Presently he will come over.'

Presently was a strange word to use: but while it lasted the Legate blessed, marked boats by the score, by the hundred, with holy water; and finally after an immense thunder of drums he told the assembly that the ceremony had been accomplished: they might now sail with God: It was as much a dismissal as *Ita, missa est*; but although something like silence came down upon the bay almost no one moved. They stood watching the Legate's splendid barge as it pulled straight across to the *Surprise*. The Legate came up the side like a right seaman and hurried across the deck to his father. 'Dearest Sam, you have not changed,' said Jack as they clasped hands. Then Sam knelt and patted his father's feet, a gesture as natural as the sun.

Then Stephen led his men forward, and they all kissed the Legate's ring. 'We must go,' said Sam, lifting his ear to a distant bell. 'But, sir, may I beg for my supper tonight?'

'I shall look forward to it extremely,' said Jack, and he went below while he could still do so with a decent composure.

IN THE CLOSE-PACKED community that made up the crew of a man-of-war there was extremely little privacy: they ate, slept, washed, relieved themselves in public; in public they were flogged, unless they happened to be officers – and in that case a severe admonition was very soon made known throughout the ship. Each man and boy knew exactly what the others earned and how much the married men sent home. And although the officers sometimes had private means, and were sometimes unwilling to speak of them, they also had servants, who knew whether their masters were bearing hard up for Poverty Bay or spreading all canvas for Port Lavish itself. The paternity orders that had brought many hands aboard were the subject of often-repeated wit.

There were few Surprises therefore who were much astonished at the very strong resemblance between the Nuncio and his host. It was perfectly well known that the younger man was one of Mr Midshipman Aubrey's indiscretions when, as a long-legged youth, he had served on the South African station, and that the boy, brought up by Catholic missionaries in Mozambique, had presented himself to his father in the West Indies, bearing the present of a charm, a ju-ju, from his affectionate mother, that had kept Jack alive through some really desperate encounters. Killick was of course a fount and a reasonably honest fount of information, much of it derived from Barret Bonden, Jack's coxswain and valued friend until he was killed in battle, a source of much greater value.

From this general history, therefore, what newcomers there were in that long harbour-watch, learnt that the good fathers, having taught Sam his letters and a considerable amount of Latin – the English he picked up with no sort of trouble – destined him for the minor orders: for nothing more, because of his illegitimate birth. But Stephen Maturin who, though a bastard himself, was very well-connected, obtained a dispensation for the young man, to whom he was particularly attached: and Sam had risen very fast indeed. To be sure, he was unusually intelligent and exceptionally good-natured: but he was also very black, shining black. And this was a time when a strong current of opinion in the Church felt that the rapidly increasing black world should be given very much more attention. On the merely practical side, the very, very large number of black

In the close-packed communities that made up the crew of a man-of-war there was extremely little privacy: they ate, slept, washed, relieved themselves in public; in public they were flogged unless they happened to be officers, and a severe admonition was very soon known throughout all the ship. Each man or boy knew exactly what the others earned and how much the married men sent home. And although the officers sometimes had private means, and were sometimes unwilling to speak of them, they also had servants, who knew whether their masters were bearing hard up, bearing hard up for Poverty Bay or spreading all canvas for Port Lavish itself. The paternity orders which had brought many hands about men

There were few surprises therefore who were much astonished at the very strong similarity between the Nuncio and his host. It was perfectly well known that the younger man was one of Mr Midshipman Aubrey's indiscretion when, as a long-legged youth, he had served on the South African station, and that the boy, brought up by Catholic missionaries in Mozambique had presented himself to his father in the West Indies, bearing the present of a heathen charm, a ju-ju, that had kept Jack alive through some really desperate encounters. Killick was of course a fount and a reasonably honest fount, of information, much of it derived from Barrett Bonden, Jack's coxswain and intimate three out of mind, a source of much greater value.

From this general history, therefore, what newcomers there were in this long harbour-watch, it learnt that the good fathers having taught Sam his letters — the language he picked up with no sort of trouble, and a considerable amount of Latin, destined him for the minor orders — but — for nothing more, because of his illegitimate birth: but Stephen Maturin who though a bastard himself was very well connected indeed and he observed a despondency for the young man, to whom he was much attached, and Sam had risen with extraordinary speed. To be sure, he was very intelligent and very good-natured; but he was also very black, shining black; and this was a time when a strong current of opinion in the Church felt that the influence of a rapidly increasing black world should receive marked notice. On the merely practical side, the very, very large number of black

men and women, slaves of or hired labourers, particularly in South America, must necessarily influence the balance of power in time. Father Panda, who was a natural-born linguist, had already done excellent work in Brazil; and now he was sent to the Argentine with greetings, and perhaps some good advice to those who were, or who were about to be, in power.

man and women, slaves or hired labourers, particularly in
South America, must necessarily influence the balance of power
in them. Father Panda, who was a natural-born linguist,
had already done excellent work in Brazil; and so now he
was sent to the Argentine with greetings, and perhaps some good
advice to those who were, or who were about to be, in power.

CHAPTER TWO

'M Y G O D, that was a damned good dinner,' said Captain Aubrey, rather loud, as though he were addressing the mast-head. He was not referring to his own meal with Sam, though that had been a capital feast in the naval style, ending with a truly sublime spotted dog, one at each end of the table, and improbable quantities of port. No: this was a physically far more gorgeous entertainment, a dinner given by the Governor in honour of His Excellency the Most Reverend Doctor Samuel Mputa (he had kept his mother's name), Papal Nuncio to the Republic of the Argentine, whose government he and his allies had undoubtedly saved very recently indeed, when a numerous body of influential moderates, together with their black followers, had defected from those who were about to break out into open rebellion, and had betrayed their arsenals. It was a dinner of high ceremony, served on gold plate of more than ordinary magnificence, with some particularly valued dishes, such as the River Plate lobster in a bitter chocolate sauce, and seventy of the finest guinea-pigs ever brought down from the mountains.

To be sure, it did lack something of the family atmosphere that had hovered in the frigate's great cabin, with every guest and servant aware of the relationship and wholly in favour of the young parson's seamanlike ways, to say nothing of his willingness to drink his wine. Here the connexion, though not unnoticed, was much less obvious, Jack being seated, not indeed below the salt, but very much nearer to it, then his son at the very top, on the Governor's right hand.

He uttered these fine ringing words addressed to the Nuncio, a little way below him, as he made his way cautiously down the palace steps, Killick and, absurdly, Awkward Davies hovering at no great distance – pitiless steps with no rail, very sharp edges, deep treads; and it was usual to make an inward promise of a fortnight's or even a month's pay to one's patron saint before embarking on them in the darkness.

There were only six steps to go under the high-held torches when a small fat boy thrust his way through the crowd and called out, 'Sir, oh sir, if you please! The squadron is in the gut, just stemming the tide.'

'Thank you, Mr Wells,' said Captain Aubrey; and craning his neck to peer in the direction of the gut he missed his step and fell into His Excellency's waiting arms. Davies' prodigious strength supported the double burden: they recovered their balance, and Jack, walking along quite steadily, said, 'Sam, I am so very happy. The squadron is down there in the gut, stemming the tide. Even with this breeze they will be moored here off the island by slack water, and you will see me go aboard, ha, ha, ha! Now cut along, there's a good fellow: you must get a decent night's sleep.'

Chapter II

'By God, that was a damned good dinner.' said Captain Aubrey, rather loud. as though he were addressing the mast-head. He was not referring to his meal with Sam, though that too had been a capital feast, in the naval style. ending with sublime spotted dog. one at each end of the table, and improbable quantities of port. No: there was a physically far more gorgeous entertainment. a dinner given by the Governor in honour of his Excellency. the Most Reverend Doctor Samuel M'Pula (he kept his mother's name). Papal Nuncio to the Republic of the Argentine. whose government Sam and his allies had saved very recently indeed ⊛ — a dinner served a gold plate of more than ordinary splendour. with some particularly valued dishes. such as/River Plate lobster served in a bitter chocolate sauce. and some of the finest guinea-pigs ever brought down from the mountains

To be sure, it lacked some of the family atmosphere that hovered about a forgaloe great cabin, with every guest and servant perfectly aware of the relationship and wholly in favour of the young parson's seamanlike ways & his willingness to drink his wine. Here the connection, though not unnoticed. was much less obvious. Jack being seated not indeed below the salt but very much nearer to it than his

He uttered these few ringing words as he made his way cautiously down the palace steps. Killick & absurdly Awkward Davis hovering at no great distance — palace steps: no rail. very sharp edge. deep treads. It was usual to make an inward promise to one's patron saint of a fortnight's or even a month's pay before embarking upon them.

Only six steps to go under the high-held torches & a small fat boy burst through the crowd and called 'Sir. oh sir: the squadron is in the gut. just slewing the tide.'

'Thank you, Mr Wells.' said Captain Aubrey: he missed his slip and fell into His Excellency's waiting arms. Davis's prodigious strength supported the double burden. they recovered their balance. and face. walking along quite steadily. said. 'Sam. I am so very happy. the squadron is slamming the tide in the gut. Even with this breeze they will be here off the island by slack water. and you will see me go aboard. ha. ho. ha.' Now cut along. there's a good fellow: you must get a decent night's sleep.'

when a numerous body of influential moderates. together with their black followers. defected from those about to break into open rebellion and betrayed their arsenals,

A decent night's sleep: there were not many people aboard the frigate who had the least expectation of such a thing. *Surprise* had three mastheads, and all were firmly occupied by the nimblest, most far-sighted young men on her books, quite irrespective of rank, and they called down every movement of their distant friends together with the even more portentous news of faintly discerned sails far down the immense estuary, conceivably the main squadron under the orders of the commander-in-chief, South African station, Lord Leyton. The *Surprise* and her tender *Ringle* would soon come under the very close, very knowing inspection of at least one senior flag-officer and of the less authoritative but sometimes even more wounding scrutiny of large numbers of officers and above all of ratings; and there was nobody aboard either of the vessels who wished his own to be mocked, fleered at or called a second-hand mud-scow. They wanted no advice on cleanliness, seamanlike appearance or the priddying of decks, no facetious observations about their attire; and even the watch below spent much of their precious sleeping-time beautifying themselves and the ship. Perhaps the most active was Killick: Captain Aubrey had served as a commodore, so he already possessed a rear-admiral's uniform: these garments had been a great source of joy to Killick, but an even greater source of anxiety – termites in Malaysia, a shameless wombat in New South Wales, while from south of the Horn to the trackless wastes of the pampas innumerable forms of vermin had gnawed or attempted to gnaw the superfine broadcloth or ruin the gold lace with their squalid dejections. During this anxious night, with so many of his shipmates scouring

The squadron is storming the tide in the gut. Even with the breeze they will be moored here off the island by slack water. and you will see me go aboard, ho. ho. ha! Now cut along. there's good fellows: you must get a decent night's sleep.

A decent night's sleep: there were not many people aboard the frigate who had the least expectation of such a thing. Surprise had only three mast-heads. but all these were firmly occupied by the nimblest most far of sighted young men on her books. quite irrespective of rank, and they called down every movement together with the ever more portentous news of faulty directed sail far down in the estuary judged to be the ~~of the South African squadron~~ other two squadrons ~~belonging to the command~~ under the authority of the Commander-in-chief of the South African station. The Surprise and her tender Ringle would come under the very close, very knowing inspection of at least two senior admirals, and there was nobody aboard either who wished her vessel to be noticed. jeered at or called a second hand mud-scow. They would need no advice on cleanliness, seamlike appearance. the or the swabbing of decks, no facetious observations about their attire; and even the watch below spend most of their precious sleepy time smartening themselves & the ship. Perhaps the most active was Killick: He ~~was in charge~~ ~~~~ Captain Aubrey had ~~already~~ served as a commodore. so he already possessed a rear-admiral's uniform: these garments had been a great source of joy to Killick. but an even greater source of anxiety — termites in Malaysia. a shameless wombat in New South Wales. from south of the Horn to the trackless wastes of the Kalahari Desert had gnawed or attempted to gnaw this superfine broadcloth and ~~desecrate~~ the gold lace with their ~~too~~ dejection. ~~During~~ this anxious vigil. with so many of her shipmates scouring

as well as the less authoritative but sometimes even more wounding scrutiny of a large number of officers & above all Tom.

pissdales or polishing musket-cocks, begging valuable slush from the cook or (more fruitfully) from his mates to give the round-shot something of a gleam as they lay along in the garlands by the great guns – during this active time he sat in the remarkably well-lit space where the surgeons often dissected their specimens or skinned their birds, sat there with Jack's best, rarely-used sea-chest open before him, half its contents spread out on a piece of sailcloth. His face was as pale as it could be, and it expressed not only horror but anguish too: for this strong clear light showed that his zeal in earlier, darker times had robbed the cloth of all its bloom. In places it was threadbare; and the heap of clothes had something of the sad, abandoned air so evident in the second-hand barrows of Monmouth Street.

'Pass the word for Killick,' called a voice from the quarterdeck, and the cry was repeated until it echoed from the open chest itself. Automatically the steward obeyed. 'Sir,' he said faintly to the towering captain.

'Have you laid out my number one uniform?'

'Well, sir, in a manner of speaking,' said Killick. 'Which it ain't what you might call weathered very well.'

Jack had never seen his steward so deeply moved. 'Be damned to that,' he said. 'Every God-damned thing in that chest was frozen stiff week after week, off the Horn. Just look out my ribbon of the Bath, will you? It sets off an old coat very well.'

'Beg pardon, sir,' said the officer of the watch. '*Suffolk* is launching a boat.'

Very true. Her barge was lowered down in a commendable fashion and manned: her acting-captain took his place by the midshipman in the stern. They pulled across with a particular accuracy of stroke and the coxswain brought her kissing alongside with barely an impact.

Captain Simmons came aboard nimbly in spite of his packet

for procedures and polishing musket cocks, begging much-valued steel from the cook or (more frightfully) her mates to give the ~~round shot~~ cannon-balls something of a gleam as they lay along in the shot-garlands by the guns — during this active time he sat in the remarkably well-lit space where the surgeons often dissected their specimens or skinned their birds, sat there with Jack's best & rarely-used sea-chest open before him, half its contents spread out on a piece of sailcloth. His face was as grave as it could be, and it expressed not only horror but anguish too: for this brilliance showed that his zeal in earlier, much darker times had robbed the cloth of all its bloom. In places it was threadbare: the heap of clothes had something of the ~~~~ overwornness the sad limp air so evident ~~in~~ Monmouth Street ~~or the barrows~~

'Pass the word for Killick' called a voice from the ~~quarterdeck~~ the second-hand barrow and the cry was repeated the length and breadth of the ship until it echoed from the open chest itself

'Sir?' he said faintly to the Authority eh captain.

'Have you laid out my number one uniform?'

'Well, in a manner of speaking,' said Killick. 'Which it ain't what you might call wethered very well —

'Be damned to that,' he said ~~said Jack~~. 'It was frozen stiff week after week off the Horn. Just look at my ribbon of the Bath, will you? It sets off an old coat very well.

'Beg pardon, sir,' said the officer of the watch. 'Sutlock is launching a boat —'

Very true. Her barge was lowering down in a seamanlike manner and manned: her acting-captain took his place in the midshipman in the stern. They pulled across with particular accuracy and the coxswain brought her alongside with perfectly accuracy —

Captain Simmons came aboard nimbly in spite of his packet

of letters. He saluted the quarterdeck and said, 'Good morning, sir. I thought you would like these' – holding up the bundle – 'as soon as possible.'

'Good morning, Simmons – a very good morning to you – how pleasant to see you again. You could not have judged better. We have had no news from home this many a day. Such a welcome packet: thank you very much indeed.'

'Not at all, sir. Do you choose to come back in *Suffolk*'s barge with your own coxswain?'

'Thank you, Simmons, but I think I shall shift my clothes, look through the chief of these papers and then come across at about four bells.'

AT THE FOURTH STROKE he ran down to the sadly weather-beaten boat where his coxswain was already sitting in the bows with his precious burden – ran down looking very grave. The red ribbon of his order shone in the light as he came aboard the *Suffolk*, but his face was as grave as ever: this was a profoundly serious occasion and he scarcely smiled as Simmons presented his officers.

This ceremony over, he nodded to his coxswain, standing there by the mizzen, and said, 'Heave out the flag.'

The folded bundle soared aloft, followed with the utmost concentration by all hands: at exactly the right moment, the exact height to an inch, the coxswain snapped the tie and the rear-admiral's blue flag streamed out bravely in the wind, instantly greeted by the first of thirteen solemn guns, enormously loud, salutes from all the members of the blue squadron, distant cheering from *Surprise* and clouds of wheeling, discontented gulls.

'May I suggest a tour of the flagship, sir?' asked Simmons, with what cheerfulness he could muster; and together they paced along the decks, through the heady scent of powder, watched with discreet intensity by all who could decently do so and by some who could not.

of letters. He saluted the quarterdeck and said 'Good morning, sir:
I thought you would like these' — holding up his packet — 'as
soon as possible.'

'Good morning Sciwmons — a very good morning to you — how
pleasant to see you again. You could not have judged better:
we have had no news from home this many a day. Such a welcome
packet: thank you very much indeed.'

'Not at all, sir. Do you choose to come back on of Suffolk's
barge with your coxswain?'

'Thank you. But I think I shall shift my clothes, look through
the chief of these, and then come across at about five bells.'

At the last stroke he ran down to the sadly weather-worn boat
where his coxswain had already settling in the bows with his precious
burden, ran down looking very grave. The red ribbon of his
order shone in the light as he came aboard the Suffolk. but his
face was as grave as ever. there was a profoundly serious occasion
and he scarcely smiled as Summons presented his officer

The ceremony over, he nodded to his coxswain. standing there
by the mizzen. and said 'Heave out the flag.'

The precious bundle soared aloft. followed with intense concentration
by all hands: at exactly the right moment. to exact height to an
inch. The coxswain snapped the tie and the rear-admiral's blue flag
streamed out bravely in the wind. instantly greeted by the first of
thirteen solemn guns. enormously loud, & salutes from all the
members of the blue squadron, and distant cheering from Suffolk.
and clouds of uneasy seagulls complaining

'May I suggest a tour of the flagship, sir?' asked Sciwmons,
with what smile he could manage, and, together they walked
along the decks, with their heavy scent of powder, watched with
discreet intensity by all who could decently do so & some who did not.

'Tell me, Simmons,' said Jack as they left the main magazine, walking delicately, as well they might with so many tons of gunpowder just behind them, 'does the Admiral sail with a flag-captain?'

'He did,' said Simmons, embarrassed. 'But Captain Fielding is going home with me if *Surprise* can find room for us both.'

'Ah,' said Jack, aware that his question was untimely. 'I only asked because I thought he might answer some of my less important questions – an admiral has plenty to do without being pestered. Perhaps I might turn to his secretary.'

'I am afraid that would scarcely answer. Poor Coulter had been hauled over the coals before now for exceeding his office . . . it is very like what you and I knew aboard *Pegasus*.'

'Oh, indeed?' That had been a short, unhappy cruise when Jack was lent to the ship to take the place of her third lieutenant, shot through the head while attempting to board a Frenchman, *Pegasus* being a ship in which most people seemed to spend their time doing wrong. 'Is not *Suffolk* somewhat shorthanded?' he asked, partly to change the subject but more to learn how a ship of the line could manage with so few people: the 'tween-decks were scarcely populated.

He did not learn, because the purser's clerk, an odd long-legged spectacled man devoured by curiosity, wished to find out who Captain Aubrey was, what he was doing here, and whether they would be able to water today or tomorrow – the great casks and hoses were all laid along – and as he uttered his almost mechanical questions, so he peered eagerly with his red-rimmed short-sighted eyes into Captain Aubrey's face, apparently devoid of shame. By the time his appetite, his very considerable appetite, was satisfied they had forgotten the shortage of hands and they walked on.

It was a long inspection and in the course of it Jack met almost all his new officers again, a seamanlike set of men on the whole, and cautiously welcoming – one or two former shipmates, known long ago. But he received a general impression of anxiety and overwork, an impression that was in part overlaid by his meeting with the gunner, the master-gunner, among his twenty-four-pounders, all as trim as heavy cannon could well be and all equipped with shining Douglas sights.

A long inspection, and by the end of it, when they stood there together in the bows, gazing out towards the approaching but still distant squadron Jack had come to like his anxious, somewhat hag-ridden companion well enough to ask, 'In really heavy weather, have you not found it difficult to work the ship with so small a company?'

'I have indeed: and I have heard of it, I do assure you . . .' He was cut short by a hail from the masthead and a moment

with its alkaline. it intelligent gunner and
his deadly copper-hooped barrels of powder in
another area

'Tell me, Simmons.' said Jack as they left the main magazine, walking
delicately, as well they might, 'does the Admiral sail with a flag-captain?'

'He did.' said Simmons, embarrassed, 'but Captain Fielding is
going home with me if Eurotas can find room for us.'

'Ah,' said Jack, aware that his question was untimely. 'I only
asked because I thought he might answer my less important question –
an admiral has plenty to do without being pestered. Perhaps I
might turn to his secretary.

'That would surely answer. Poor Condler has been hauled over the coals
for exceeding his office ... it is very like what you and I knew aboard
~~Hermione~~ ~~Hermione~~ Pegase.

'Oh, indeed?'. That had been a short, unhappy cruise. When Jack
was lent to the ship to take the place of her third lieutenant – shot through
the head: a ship in which most people seemed to spend their time doing
wrong. 'It is not Suffolk somewhat short-handed?' asked Jack
partly to change the subject ~~and~~ ~~but more~~ I learn how a ship of the
line could manage with her so few people: the lower-decks was scarcely
populated

It was a long inspection, and in the course of it Jack met almost all
his new officers. a seaman-like set of men upon the whole. and courteous
welcoming – one or two former shipmates, known long ago. But Jack
received a general impression of anxiety and overwork, an impression
that was soon in part overlaid by his meeting with the gunner. His master-gunner
among his lower-decks gun-decks 24 lbrs. all as trim as heavy cannon can
well be and all equipped with Douglas sights.

A long inspection and by the end of it, when they stood there together
in the bow, gazing out towards the effectually but still distant squadron.
Jack had come to love his answers. somewhat hag-ridden companion will
enough to ask. 'Has in heavy weather, have you not found it difficult
the ship, so short-handed as she is?'.

'I have indeed: and I have heard of it. I assure you...'
He was cut short by a hail from the mast-head and a moment

later the message came forward: the rear-admiral was desired to go aboard the flag.

'I am afraid it will be a wet pull,' said Simmons. 'May I lend you a tarpaulin jacket?'

'If you please,' said Jack: his fine but aged uniform had not much wear left in it and he was a long, long way from home.

A wet pull it was, through an increasingly choppy sea, right into the eye of the wind: it was however shortened by the zeal of the white and blue squadrons to reach a hospitable port.

'Well, Aubrey,' said the Admiral, looking at him with a certain satisfaction, 'You have had a wet time of it, I see. You should have put on an oilskin: still, we cannot all be wise all the time. I have called you out so far from shore because there are two questions I should like to settle. The first is supplies. We are very low in everything – tobacco is quite gone – and all the way down my pursers, agents and so on have had the utmost difficulty with the locals, even in ports where we have always been welcomed and entertained. Difficulties about water, difficulties about cattle . . . even about shore-leave and common supplies – no bumboats coming off, no whores. What is it like with you in Buenos Aires? Should I push on? Things are desperate low and with the present ministry I dare not use force. How are things with you?'

'My lord, until a few days ago we had great difficulty in getting supplies of any kind, but then an eminent ecclesiastic, a Papal Nuncio particularly well known to my political adviser Dr Maturin . . .'

'Yes, yes. Sr Joseph mentioned him to me: I shall pay him some attention.'

'. . . came in and now everything is settled. We lack for nothing, and prices are very moderate. We are amply stored for the Cape, and *Surprise*, which is now bound for home with my dispatches, is in much the same case.'

'I am heartily glad to hear of it. That will be a very great relief.' Lord Leyton uttered these words, but his aged yellow face did not match them at all. His expression remained discontented, querulous, ready to find fault or to contradict. However he did say, '*Surprise*: yes, that reminds me.

& later the message came forward: the rear-admiral was desired to go aboard th flag.

'I am afraid it will be a wet pull.' said Simmons. 'May I lend you a tarpaulin jacket?'

'If you please,' said Jack. His fine but aged uniform had not much wear left in it and he was a long, long way from home

A wet pull it was through an increasingly choppy sea, right into the eye of the wind: it was however shortened by the zeal of the white and the red squadrons to reach a hospitable port

'Well, Aubrey,' said the Admiral, looking at him with a certain satisfaction. 'you have had a wet pull of it, I see. You should have put on an (— as much as his discontented face could express —) oil-skin. Well, we cannot all be wise all the time. I have called you out so far because there are two questions that I wish to settle. The first is supplies. We are very low in everything — tobacco is quite gone — and all the way down my pursers, agents and so on have had the utmost difficulty with th locals, even in ports where we have always been welcomed and entertained. ~~Difficulties~~ Difficulties about water. difficulties about cables ... even about common shore supplies — no bum-boats coming off, no whores. What is it like with you in Buenos Aires? Should I push on, do you think? Things are desperate low and with the present ministry in power I dare not use force. How are things with you?'

'My lord, until a few days ago we had great difficulties in getting supplies of any kind, but then an eminent ecclesiastic, a Papal Nuncio particularly well known to my political adviser, Dr Maturin ...'

'Yes, yes: Sir Joseph mentioned him to me. I shall pay him some marked attention.'

'... came in, and now everything is settled. We lack for nothing, and prices are very moderate. We are amply stored for th Cape, and Surprise, which is now bound for home with my dispatches, is in much the same case.'

'I am heartily glad to hear it. That will be a very great relief.' Lord Leyton uttered these words, but his aged yellow face did not match them at all. His expression remained discontented, querulous, readier to find faults or to contradict. However, he did say 'Surprise: yes, that reminds me

One of the reasons that I asked you to come out was to tell you that I intend to send two of my officers home in her and to ensure that there should be no trouble about taking them and an unsatisfactory midshipman aboard your vessel.'

'You will forgive me, my lord, but *Surprise* is no longer my vessel. To be sure, I did command her, but she was on hire to the Hydrographical Department of the Admiralty until I should meet your squadron, hoist my flag and take up my new appointment. The moment I did that, *Surprise's* contract with the Admiralty came to an end. She returns to the sole ownership of her proprietor, a free agent. If you wish I will ask him whether he chooses to take these people aboard: but it is entirely at his discretion. He is at no man's command.'

'What a damned hair-splitting sea-lawyer you are, upon my word, Aubrey,' cried the Admiral. 'You can damned well go back to that half-baked privateerly donkey-frigate and give the owner my orders to take these two officers and the reefer aboard. If he makes the slightest demur or objection tell him that I shall press every man in his ship and leave him to wallow in the mud of the River Plate until she rots.' At this point the Admiral's yellow face had a curious flush and his eyes fairly blazed: one clenched fist rose and fell.

'*The slightest demur or objection . . . shall press every man . . .*' repeated Jack, rising and drawing his tarpaulin round him.

'Awkward, legalistic, cavilling sod . . .' muttered the Admiral: and then, more audibly, as he rang for his steward, 'Sit down, sit down, and drink some madeira to the squadron's supplies. Amphlett' – to the steward – 'the decanter of madeira from the coach: and a couple of glasses.' A pause, and he went on, 'I do not like to ask a political adviser to come out in this blow – the doctor physicked Prince William, did he not? I am told he is very well with His Highness. But if you would tell him that you have explained the situation and that I should take it as a personal favour if he would allow these people to go aboard his ship, I should be obliged to you.'

'Very good, sir. Now if I may I shall carry your message to Dr Maturin: if I were to take your purser and perhaps your secretary back with me to *Surprise*, my people could tell them all we know about our plentiful,

One of the reasons that I asked you to come out here was to tell you that I wished to send two of my officers home in her and to ensure that there should be no trouble about taking them and an unsatisfactory midshipman aboard your vessel.

'You will forgive me, my lord, but Surprise is no longer my vessel. She was on hire to the Hydrographical Department of the Admiralty until I should meet you _To be sure I did command her, but_ ; hoist my flag and _take up_ assume my new appointment. The moment I have done that, Surprise's contract with the Admiralty terminates: she returns to the ownership of her proprietor, a free agent. If you wish I will ask him if he chooses to take these people aboard; but it is entirely at his discretion. He is at no man's command.'

'What a damned hair-splitting sea-lawyer you are, upon my word, Aubrey,' cried the Admiral. 'You can damned well go back to that half-baked privateering donkey, forget, and give the owner my orders to take these two officers and the reefer aboard. If he makes the slightest demur or objection tell him that I shall press every man in his ship and leave him to wallow in the mud of the River Plate until she rots.' At this point the Admiral's yellow face bore on a curious flush and his eyes fairly blazed; one clenched old foot rose & fell.

'The _slightest demur or objection ... shall press every man..._' repeated Jack, rising and drawing her _Captain_ toward him.

'Awkward, legalistic, cavilling sod...' muttered the Admiral; and then, more audibly, as he rang for his steward. 'Sit down; sit down, and drink some madeira to the squadron's supplies. Amphlett' – to the steward – 'the decanter of madeira from the coach; and a couple of glasses.' A pause, and he went on. 'I do not like to set a political adviser to come out in this blow – the Doctor physicked Prince William, did he not?*– but if you would tell him that you have explained the situation and that I should take it as a personal favour if he would take these people aboard his ship.'

'Very good, sir. Now, if I may, I shall carry your message to Dr Maturin; & if I were to take your packet back with me in Surprise, my people could tell him all we know about our Menelaus,

comes on p 23

* He is very well with the Prince, I am told

and perhaps ourselves

12
23
36

plentiful sources of supply. The present governor is entirely on our side, and I do not think you will be disappointed.'

'Make it so, Aubrey,' said the Admiral, rising. 'And when you dine aboard me tomorrow, pray bring your political adviser. I should be happy to be acquainted with him and to offer what civilities I can. I presume he goes home in *Surprise*?'

'I cannot tell, my lord: his mission in Chile is clearly at an end – a most satisfactory end – but there may also be some duties waiting for him in South Africa and above all eastwards. He and Dr Jacob are very knowing about those parts. But in any case I mean to return to her at once, and transfer some of her hands to poor thin *Suffolk*.'

'Aye. It was the yellow jack. Off Port of Spain.'

'And I shall carry your message. Your servant, my lord, and thank you for the capital madeira.'

The pull back had the breeze and the sea right aft, and Jack went aboard *Surprise* in fine style, the side dressed by smiling seamen and officers. He asked for the Doctor, who, unused to the ceremonies attending a flag-officer, was reading in the great cabin, reading his letters from home. Jack noticed his gravity but delivered Lord Leyton's invitation and said, 'I shall be back in a few minutes: please sort out my post and I shall join you.'

On deck he gave the not unexpected order for all hands and when the particularly attentive group was assembled he said, 'Shipmates, as you know, the barky is going home. Some people are uneasy in their minds at being thrown ashore in peace-time . . .' A general murmur of agreement: intense interest. 'Well, I can take sixty-three prime seamen over to *Suffolk* with me. Aboard her it would in course be the same pay, rations and allowances as here, and in her you would find some officers you already know and a score or two of former shipmates. So let them as choose to serve on the South African station ask my clerk to set their names down on a list and I shall mark those I think best suited for the climate.'

A general buzz of strong approval, not quite a cheer, out of respect for a flag-officer, and Rear-Admiral Aubrey plunged below, where Stephen looked up with a frown, pushing Jack's heap towards him and silently going on with his own.

Sophie Aubrey had almost all the virtues of a woman who had had

pleahful sources of supply. The present governor is entirely on our side, and I do not think you will be disappointed.

'Maybe it so

'Do that thing, Aubrey,' said the Admiral, 'Maybe so'/. 'And when you come to dine aboard me [pray bring your political adviser. I should be happy to make his acquaintance. I know him — be acquainted with him and to offer what civilities I can. (I presume to goes home in Surprise ?)

'Just so, my lord: and indeed I mean to return to her at once, to transfer some of her hands to poor men Suffolk ~

'Aye. It was the yellow Jack.' of Port of Spain

'And I shall carry your message Your servant, my lord, and thank you for the Capital Madeira.

The wind back, with the breeze and the sea right aft, and Jack went aboard Surprise in fine style, the side dressed by smiling seamen and officers. He went asked for the Doctor, who, immune to these ceremonies was reading in the great cabin, reading his letters from home. Jack noticed his serious look, delivered his invitation. and said 'I shall be back in a few minutes : please sort out my post & I shall join you:

 On deck he give the. expected not unexpected order for all hands and when the particularly attentive group was assembled he said 'Shipmates, as you know. the barky is going home Some people are uneasy in their minds about being thrown ashore in peace-time.' A general murmur of agreement: intense interest. 'Well. I can take 63 prime seamen with me. Aboard Suffolk it would in course be the same pay. rations & allowances as here, and in her you would find some officers you already know and a score or two of former shipmates So let them that choose to serve of the South African station ask my clerk to set their names down on a list and I shall mark those I think best suited for the climate:

 A general buzz of strong approval, not quite a cheer. out of respect for a flag-officer, and Rear-Admiral Aubrey plunged off below. where Stephen looked up with a frown. pushing Jack's heap towards him and going on with his own. silently

 Sophie Aubrey had almost all the virtues of a woman who had had

MS g p 9 is written on the back of ⑪ p 6

the meagre education of her class, taught by a singularly ignorant governess – little beyond the three R's and a smattering of French together with a list of good and bad kings. She had never been encouraged to read and in fact she had read very little; but she could and did write a singularly beautiful hand. Her piano-playing was purely mechanical, yet then again she had naturally pretty manners, she was tall and slim, her complexion was quite admirable and she moved with a perfect, unconscious grace – it was a delight to see her going down the dance. But she was an indifferent, unwilling horsewoman in spite of arduous, dreaded lessons in her youth and her husband's kindly-meant encouragement: and she had never learnt to date her letters.

Jack's bundle had not come aboard arranged in order of time and although from a few hints thrown out by chance – gifts of partridges, the flowering of certain shrubs, children's holidays, birthday feasts – he slowly imposed a remote hint of sequence he could scarcely confide in it at all. He did make out that his valuable agent was managing his more distant estate – the inherited rotten borough that gave him a seat in Parliament – remarkably well, that the Woolcombe land was more prosperous than ever it had been, and that generally speaking the children's health, apart from the usual coughs, colds and one greenstick fracture, was all that could be wished.

The pattern, the history of all that these many letters told, was still very far from clear, but the hint of discord and unhappiness that he had acquired from the first random pages and that he had carried with an anxious mind to the *Suffolk* – the hint that had much increased the gravity of that ceremony – now expanded to a conscious and reasoned certainty: there had indeed been grave unhappiness at Woolcombe, and in all likelihood the unhappiness was still there.

From time to time he glanced over at Stephen, who was equally grave, but whose letters – whose dated and indeed numbered letters (for from early childhood Christine had been brought up to keep exact ornithological and botanical records) were now assembled in neatly-ordered piles that he was at present annotating in a private script, just as he would have annotated any other body of intelligence documents. From time to time Stephen felt his friend's gaze heavy upon him; but this was an exceedingly delicate affair, with very strong emotions involved, and he did not choose to broach a subject that concerned Jack even more than it concerned him: still less did he wish to force a confidence. He therefore made no observation of any kind until Jack turned

singularly a miserable history of good roys & bad
? laid it by a singulair ignorant governess

very little education beyond the three Rs and a smattering of French,
one who had never been encouraged to read and who in fact had read very
little : but she could and did write a singularly beautiful hand. Her piano-
playing was purely mechanical, yet on the other hand she was tall, slim,
her complexion was quite admirable and she moved with a perfect, unconscious
grace — it was a delight to see her going down the dance. but yet she was a
very poor unwilling & horsewoman in spite of arduous, dreaded lessons in
her youth and her husband's kindly-meant encouragement; and she had
never learnt to date her letters

Jack's bundle had never not com been brought aboard been arranged in order of time and although
from by few had thrown out by chance — & gifts of partridges, the flowering of
certain shrubs, children's holidays, — he slowly imposed a remote
semblance of hint of sequence he could scarcely confide it in it at all
He did make out that his valuable agent was managing his distant estate
& remarkably well, that the Woolcombe land was more prosperous than
ever it had been and that generally speaking the children's health, apart
from the usual coughs, colds & one greenstick fracture, was all that
could be wished.

It had had a hm The pattern, the history of all that these many
letters told was still very far from clear. but the hint of discord and
unhappiness that he had acquired from the first random letters and that
he had carried with him to the Suffolk — the hint that had much
increased the gravity of that ceremony, now expanded to a conscious
and reasoned certainty: there had been grave unhappiness
at Woolcombe, and in all likelihood there still was

From time to time he glanced over at Stephen, who was equally
grave. but whose letters — whose dates and indeed numbered letters — were now
assembled in neatly-ordered piles that he was now annotating in a
private script as he would have annotated any other body of intelligence
documents. From time Stephen felt his friend's gaze heavy upon
him; but this was an exceedingly delicate affair. with very strong
emotions involved, and he did not chose to broach a discussion subject which
concerned Jack even more than it concerned him: still less to force a
confidence. He said nothing therefore, until Jack turned to him

made no observation of any kind

and said, 'Brother, I am most uncommon stupid today, what with the emotion of hoisting my flag – hoisting my flag, God bless us all – and having a set-to with Lord Leyton as well as coping with our people – and I cannot make head or tail of what is afoot at home, except that they do not seem to be quite friends. Have you puzzled it out? I mean, if you have had the same kind of letters?'

'I believe I have, my dear, though I may well be mistaken. You will recall that Christine went down to Woolcombe at my particular request and at dear Sophie's invitation?'

'Yes, yes: I remember it perfectly.'

'At that time your twin daughters were away, at their aunt's school in Ulster.'

'Just so. They travelled with James Callaghan, whose eldest girl is there too.'

'So at Woolcombe there was just Sophie, your young George on long leave while his ship was refitting, Christine Wood and my Brigid. Edward Heatherleigh had brought them down from the North Country, but at that point he did not stay, having at least three papers to read before the Society.'

'All this while we were moving slowly down towards Brazil.'

Stephen nodded and went on, 'Perhaps I told you that among a quantity of letters that I received at Funchal there was a note from Edward speaking of his delight, in the countryside about Woolcombe and his hope of hunting there one day?'

'I believe you did. Do you think a pot of coffee would sharpen my wits?' He touched the bell. 'You will take a cup, I am sure?'

Stephen agreed and went on. 'That was the posture of affairs: a very elegant posture too, with George and Brigid excellent good friends, often riding on a stout well-boned pony – the source, alas, of that greenstick fracture.'

'It knit very soon and it earned him another three months' leave.'

'To be sure. And this was the state of affairs when Edward came back from London. He had been charmed by the reception of his papers and he was even more charmed by the countryside; he thought it

and said 'Brother, I am most uncommon stupid today, what π
with the emotion of hoisting my flag — hoisting my flag, God bless us
all — and having a set-to with Lord Layton as well as coping
with our people — and I cannot make head or tail of what is afoot
afoot at home, except that they do not seem such friends. Have
you puzzled it out? ˄ I mean, if you have had the same kind of letters?'

'I believe I have, my dear, though I may well be mistaken. Christine
went down to Woolcombe at my particular request and at dear
Sophie's invitation.' ['You will recall that]

'Yes, yes: I remember it perfectly.'

'At that time your twin daughters were away, at their aunt's
school in Ulster.'

'Just so. They travelled with James Callaghan, whose eldest
girl is there too.'

'So at Woolcombe there were just Sophie, your young George on long
leave while his ship was being refitted, Christine Wood and my Brigid.
Edward had brought them down from the North Country but at that
point he did not stay, having at least three papers to read before the
Society.'

'All this while we were moving slowly down towards Brazil.'

'Perhaps I told you that among a quantity of letters that I received
at Funchal there was a note from Edward speaking of his delight in
the countryside about Wood Woolcombe and his hope of kindly then
one day?'

'Perhaps you do. Do you think that a pot of coffee would
sharpen my wits?' He touched the bell. 'You will take a cup,
I am sure?'

Stephen nodded and went on. 'That was the posture of affairs: a
very elegant posture too, with George & Brigid excellent good friends, often
riding on a stout well-boned pony.— the source, alas, of a greenstick
fracture.

'It knit very soon, and it earned him another three months' leave.'

'To be sure. And this was the state of affairs when Edward
came back from London. He had been charmed by the reception of
his papers and he was even more charmed by the countryside; he

ideal for fishing, for hunting fox or hare, and for recording the movements, mating, nesting and diet of an extraordinarily large number of birds, and he asserted that he should start making enquiries for a house to be let or sold, observing that although their place in the north was very well, the weather was exceptionally and increasingly severe, which his declining health could no longer endure. So Sophie, judging very rightly from his carriage, servants and evident style of living, suggested a comfortable, fair-sized house a quarter of a mile away.'

'Medenham.'

'Just so . . . which had been empty for some time, but which, with a gardens and meadows, had been carefully kept up and which was to be had at a modest rent by a tenant such as Mr Heatherleigh, and if dear Christine liked she would ask the agent for an order to view.'

The brother and sister viewed with every intention of being pleased and they came away delighted. Indeed they would have been difficult to satisfy if they had not liked Medenham, a warm, comfortable, spacious, low-built house of Charles II's time with linen-cupboards fit to shelter a troop of horses, massive furniture of another age and a considerable library, mostly of travel and natural philosophy.

The affair was soon concluded; necessaries and a few servants were sent down from the north, and the new tenants moved in; the nearby families soon paid their visits, and Mr Heatherleigh and his sister were pronounced a great acquisition to the neighbourhood, particularly as Mr Heatherleigh spoke eagerly of his intention to hunt that year.

This however proved a hope not easily realized. The horses were soon in the stalls, a handsome bay mare and two promising grey geldings, but Mr Heatherleigh had a troublesome neighbour in the north who coveted his estate and when it was refused to be sold this man turned to the exceedingly complex law governing mineral deposits in those parts which, he contended, gave him the right in the peculiar jurisdiction of the province to pursue an uninterrupted vein under the adjoining land – under Edward Heatherleigh's land. Before Michaelmas, therefore, the poor man climbed into his coach again and travelled northwards to his bitter moors through the driving rain, to spend all his diminishing

ideal for fishing, for hunting the fox or the hare, and for recording the movements,

neatly and alert of an extraordinary

large number of hear

said he should start making enquiries for a house to be let or sold.
observing that although their place in the north was very well, the
weather was exceptionally severe, which his declining health could not no longer
endure bear. So Sophia, judging very rightly from his carriage, servants
and evident style of living, at once suggested a comfortable, fair-sized house
not a quarter of a mile away...'

'Medenham.'

'Just so... which had been empty for some time, but which, with its
gardens & meadows, has been carefully kept up and which was to be
had, at a modest rent by a tenant such as Mr Edward. Woolcombe
own man of business was in charge of the matter, and if dear Mrs Wood
liked she would ask him to give them an order to view.'

They viewed with every intention of being pleased and they came away
delighted. Indeed they would have been difficult to satisfy if they had
not liked Medenham, a warm, comfortable, spacious, low-built house of Charles II's
time age with linen-cupboards to shelter a troop of horse, massive
furniture of another age and a considerable library, mostly of natural
philosophy.

The affair was soon concluded; necessaries and a few servants were
sent down from the north, and the new tenants moved in; the neighbouring
families soon paid their visits, and Mr Edward & his smaller were said
to be a great acquisition to the neighbourhood, particularly as Mr Edward
spoke eagerly of his intention to hunt that year.

This however proved a hope not easily realized. The horses were there,
a handsome bay mare and two promising grey geldings, but Mr Edward
had a troublesome neighbour in the north who coveted his estate and when
it was refused to be sold turned to the exceeding complex law
governing mineral deposits which, he contended, gave him the right, to pursue
in the peculiar jurisdiction of that province (part of the county of Durham) to
pursue an uninterrupted vein under the adjoining land. Before Michaelmas,
therefore, the poor man climbed into his coach again and travelled northwards
to his bitter moors and through the driving rain. To spend all his diminishing

under Edwards lands

energy in lawyers' meetings and vain attempts at understanding counsels' opinions on the most profoundly obscure customary laws of usage where minerals were concerned in that particular district.

During this period Christine spent much of her time at Woolcombe, and so, except for those necessary hours in the school-room with her new governess, the capable and intelligent Miss West, did Brigid, walking in and out as though it were her own home, often accompanied by her companion George, who sometimes improved his indifferent mathematics with Miss West and sometimes showed both governess and pupil the higher flights of knotting.

It was during the later part of this season when field mushrooms were to be had by the basketful for the picking that the little household began to look for the return of Mr Edward – he had uttered some general remarks about having a wheel retyred and the horses shod – when a carriage was heard coming up the drive. For a few moments those who were drinking tea in the small drawing-room thought it might possibly be Mr Edward's coach, sounding soft because of the rain: but not at all – it was a common post-chaise bringing the twins earlier than usual (not at all uncommon with Sophie's sister, who would seize upon any conveyance, any travelling-companion, to send her pupils home).

The letters that described this homecoming varied; but Stephen, who knew those concerned extremely well, saw the Aubrey girls hurrying in, tired, cross and hungry, intensely jealous at seeing Brigid sitting there by their mother, warm, prettily dressed and well-fed. 'Are you still here?' asked Charlotte. 'You are always here!' cried Fanny, and there was some motion towards pushing her off the sofa, strongly repelled by George. Clearly Sophie and Christine dealt with the situation – the clack and din of the accompanying County Armagh maidservant was a great help – and the Aubrey girls were taken away, washed and fed, while Christine led Brigid home, desiring Padeen to carry the twins' trunk indoors and settle with the postillion.

'As I see it, dear Jack,' said Stephen, 'the twins' jealousy, exacerbated by the weariness of travelling, extreme hunger and the hot squalor of a post-chaise, exploded into open violence when they saw Brigid there, brushed and in a handsome garment sitting in the most favoured place next to their mother.

energy in lawyers' meetings and vain attempts at understanding counsels' opinion on the profoundly obscure customary laws of the usage where minerals were concerned in that particular district.

During this time Christine spent much of her time at Woolcombe and, except for those necessary hours in the school-room with her new governess, the capable and intelligent Miss West, did Brigid wander in and out as if it were her own home, often accompanied by her companion George, who sometimes improved his indifferent mathematics with Miss West and sometimes showed both governess and pupil to higher flights of knitting.

It was during the later part of this season, when field mushrooms were to be had for the picking, that the little household began to look for the return of Mr Edward — he had, when he gave some general remarks about having a wheel retyred and the horses shod — when a carriage heard coming up the drive. For a few moment those who were drinking tea in the small drawing-room thought it might possibly be Mr Edward's coach, sounding soft because of the rain: but not at all — it was a common post-chaise bringing the twins earlier than usual (not at all uncommon with Sophie's sister, who would seize upon any conveyance, any travelling-companion, to send her pupils home)

The letters that described this homecoming varied, but Stephen, who knew those concerned intimately well, saw the Aubrey girls hurrying in, tired, cross and hungry, intensely jealous at seeing Brigid sitting there by their mother. 'Are you still here?' asked one, 'You are always here,' said the other, and there was some motion towards pushing her off the sofa. Clearly Sophie and Christine dealt with the situation — the noise of the accompanying manservant was a great help — and the Aubrey girls were taken away, washed and fed, while Christine led Brigid home, desiring Padeen to carry the twins' trunk indoors and to settle with postilion

'As I see it, my dear,' said Stephen, 'the twins' jealousy, exacerbated by the weariness of travelling, her extreme hunger, and the hot sight of a post-chaise, exploded into real open violence when she saw Brigid, perfectly dressed, brushed and sitting in the most favoured place next to her mother,

A good night's sleep, a body-bath of warm water, fresh clothes and a substantial breakfast is likely to restore all their amiability.'

'I am sure you are right,' said Jack, but he did not believe it. He knew, far better than Stephen, that there was little amiability to restore. Not from the beginning, when the little girls were virtually one being, but quite early, he had seen this jealousy directed by a mutual common understanding against any person, any creature even, for whom their gentle and affectionate mother showed a particular liking. Their father, being a sort of household god, was exempt, and so were some of the minor animals; but not George, who was accused of siding with Brigid against them and of running after her like a little dog.

It was an unhappy state of affairs, above all that Edward Heatherleigh was away in the north and that in his absence Christine was staying at Woolhampton, where her support for Brigid increased the atmosphere of ill-will.

'Sometimes I count the remaining days of holiday on the calendar,' write Sophie. 'They seem to stretch on and on, and I am so afraid that Christine and I may quarrel. Sometimes I see her check the angry words when the twins are particularly unkind: and rather than have that I am minded to suggest that she and Padeen should travel up to the north to stay with dear Edward, at least until the girls go back to school. I know that she is particularly anxious to escape the attentions, the very pronounced attentions, of Captain Miller.'

'I do not think I know about Captain Miller.' said Stephen. 'What is his ship?'

'Oh no: he is only a soldier,' said Jack. 'He has a moderate estate the other side of Caxley. A surprising number of pheasants; but a sad coxcomb, I fear. I only say 'How d'ye do?' when we meet. A soldier: his regiment was posted to Sierra Leone at one time. That will be the Admiral,'

A good night sleep, a body-bath of warm water, fresh clothes and a substantial breakfast is likely to restore all their amiability.'

'I am sure you are right', said Jack, but he did not believe it. He knew, far better than Stephen, that there was little amiability to restore. Not from the beginning, when the little girls were virtually one being, but (tho a male common understanding) quite early, he had seen this jealousy directed at almost any person, any creature even, for whom their gentle and otherwise mother showed a particular liking. Their father, being a sort of household god, was exempt, and so were some of the minor animals; but not George, who was accused of siding with Brigid against them and of running after her like a little dog.

It was an unhappy state of affairs, above all now that Mr Edward was away in the north and that Christine was staying at Woolhampton, where her support for Brigid increased the atmosphere of ill will.

'~~fortunately the end of the holidays is not very, very far away,' wrote Sophie, 'and then they can go back to Ulster, their school where they have such a lot of friends who are neither prettier nor cleverer or better at French than themselves~~

'Sometimes I count the remaining days of holiday on the calendar,' wrote Sophie 'They seem to stretch on and on, and I am so afraid that Christine and I may quarrel. Sometimes I see her slip the angry words when the twins are particularly unkind: and rather than have that I am minded to suggest that she and Padeen should travel up to the north to stay with dear Edward, at least until the girls go back to school. I know that she is particularly eager anxious to escape the attentions, the very pronounced attentions of Captain Miller.'

'I do not think I do know about Captain Miller,' said Stephen.

'He has a moderate estate the other side of Caxley,' said Jack. 'A surprising quantity of pheasants; but a sad coxcomb, I fear. I only say "How d'ye do?" when we meet. A sad soldier: ~~you know~~ ~~the~~ was posted to Sierra Leone at one time. That will be the Admiral,'

he said, breaking off as the salute began, doubled and redoubled by echoes and by the citadel's prodigious reply to Leyton's civility.

'The Admiral is at hand,' said Jack in the flattened silence, 'and I should have told you before that he begs the favour of passage home for his flag-captain and another unfortunate whose name I forget. And I rather think, brother, that I have pledged your word in exchange for the moving of sixty-odd prime hands to *Suffolk*, which can hardly win her anchors else. Oh, they were so happy when . . .'

'Wittles is up,' said Killick, and the scent of toasted cheese wafted in with him.

They ate in silence, intently, hungrily; and then, resting his fork, Jack said, 'I have had what I think is an idea worthy of Newton: but during the night I must spend the rest of my time reading the rest of my letters and unless they contradict me I shall tell you at breakfast: for once that is eaten, *Surprise* must make sail.'

he said as the salute began, doubled and redoubled by echoes and by the citadel's prodigious reply to Lord Leyton's civility

'The Admiral is at hand,' said Jack. 'and I should have told you before that he begs in favour of passage home for his flag-captain and another unfortunate whose name I forget. I rather think, brother, that I have pledged your word in exchange for the weary of sixty-odd ~~pounds~~ from hands to Suffolk, which can hardly win her anchors else. Oh, they were so happy when...

'Kettle is up,' said Killick, and the scent of toasted cheese wafted in with him.

They ate in silence, intently, hungrily, and then setting his fork, Jack said 'I have had what I think is an idea worth of Newton: but during the night I could read the rest of my

 unless

bullies a ~~would they contradict~~ contradict me I shall tell you at breakfast: for once that is eaten. Suppressment wrecke said.

CHAPTER THREE

THE DIMINISHED but still well-manned *Surprise* and her lithe fore-and-aft companion *Ringle* swung easily at their moorings on the making tide not far from the imposing *Suffolk*, and they gazed at the South African squadron farther inshore, actively victualling, watering and getting ready to move into various docks and yards beyond the citadel for repairs, some of them urgent.

'Good morning, Stephen,' said Jack as his friend walked into the cabin.

'Good morning to you, my dear,' said Stephen.

'You have done your writing, I see?'

'So I have too: a simple harsh direction that Brigid shall be delivered into the hands of the bearer and carried aboard – whichever vessel we decide upon – there to be in her father's custody: this is, as I understand it, a necessary legal form in case any of Diana's relatives should object. It is, I hope entirely softened by a most affectionate private note to Christine and her brother, inviting them to join us.'

'I have done much the same, simply requiring Sophie to come aboard with the utmost dispatch, bringing a minimum of impediments, and of course the girls.'

Each eyed the other's letter, which looked more like a laboured study than a simple note; and Jack said, 'Well, let us at least have a preliminary cup, and then we can ask Harding to join us.' Some moments later he touched the bell, and said to Killick, 'Ask Mr Harding to walk in. Mr Harding, pray sit down – may I pour you a cup of coffee? Now you know very well that *Surprise* and *Ringle* are to return to Portsmouth with all possible speed to deliver a certain number of officers to the Commander-in-Chief, together with the Doctor's communications and my dispatches. You may find it possible to shape your course without any impropriety so that you touch at Shelmerston before heading for Plymouth. If it is feasible, you, a firm-natured married man, will post straight to Woolcombe and there hand this letter to my wife and this to Mrs Wood, her near neighbour. Our hope, do you see, is to convey both ladies, together with Mrs Wood's brother, the three children

Chapter III

The diminished but still well-manned Surprise and her litho fore-and-aft rigged companion Ringle swung easily at their moorings on the making tide. not far from the imposing Suffolk, and they gazed at the South African squadron farther inshore, actively victualling, watering and getting ready to move into various docks and yards beyond the citadel for repairs, some of them urgent.

'Good morning. Stephen.' said Jack as his friend walked into the cabin.

'Good morning to you. my dear.' said Stephen

'You have done your writing. I see?.

'So I have too: a simple harsh [direction] requirement that Bridget shall be delivered into the hands of the bearer to be carried aboard — whatever vessel we decide upon; this is, I understand a necessary legal form in case any of Diana's relatives should object. It is, I hope, entirely softened by a most affectionate private note to Christine and her brother, inviting them to join us.

'I have done much the same. simply requesting Sophie to come aboard with the utmost despatch. bringing a minimum of impedimenta. and a cousin this guide.

Each eyed the other's letter. which looked more like a laboured essay than a simple note; & then Jack said 'Well. let us at least have a preliminary cup, & then we can ask Harding to join us.' Some moments later he touched the bell. and said to Killick 'Ask Mr Harding to walk in. Mr Harding. pray sit down — may I pour you a cup of coffee?. Now you know very well that Surprise & Ringle are to return to Portsmouth with all possible despatch speed to deliver to deliver a certain number of officers, to its C-in-C. together with the doctor's messages & my despatches. You may find it possible to shape your course so that you touch at Shelmerston without any impropriety before heading for Plymouth. If it is feasible you. . from. matured married men. will post straight over to Woolcombe & there hand this letter to my wife. and this to Mrs Maturin. her new neighbour. Our hope. do you see. is to [convey] carry both ladies, the three children.

together with Mr Wood's booklies.

and the strict minimum of attendants to the Cape, either catching the squadron before it leaves the River Plate or joining company during the voyage – they will almost certainly water at Saint Helena – or simply at the Cape itself. Now you know both vessels through and through; and you know more than I do about children, attendants and the married state. When you have heard the ladies express their views on baggage and on these points you will form an opinion on the irreducible minimum and choose your conveyance accordingly. *Ringle* is undoubtedly faster than *Surprise*, but I should not like to have her pasengers unduly cramped – given a disgust of the sea – for the sake of a few days.'

'Two ladies, one gentleman, three children, and I suppose three or four maids and a man.'

'It does of course depend on whether the gentleman chooses to come,' observed Jack. 'Mr Harding, you will read these letters if you please: they are in no way confidential.'

'I make no doubt that the gentleman will come,' said Stephen.

Harding, a poised middle-aged lieutenant, read the letters with attention. The others watched him. 'Well, sir,' he said at last, 'Well, gentlemen: I am of opinion that *Ringle* is the right choice. I was perpetually easing my sheet when she was in company with *Surprise*, though indeed there are few faster frigates. The passengers will not lie altogether at their ease, to be sure, but they will have the delight of seeing the bow-wave flung wide to leeward and the wake racing away, everything alive and tearing through the water. They would be dull souls that did not love that: and if I may be so bold, Miss Brigid loved it purely last time she was afloat in a blow. Anyhow, you would want *Ringle* as a tender, sir.'

'Very true: so you think all these people could be crammed in?'

'I should take my davy on it, sir.'

'Very well. You can sail with *Surprise*, then; and she will deliver my officers, passengers and despatches at Portsmouth, then run down to be laid up in Sepping's yard, while you return with your passengers in *Ringle*.

and the strict minimum of attendants to the Cape, either catching the squadron before it leaves the River Plate, joining company during the voyage — we shall almost certainly water at St Helena — or simply at the Cape itself. Now you know both vessels through and there; and you know more than I do about children, attendants and the married state. When you have heard the ladies express their views on these points you will form an opinion on the irreducible minima & choose your vessel accordingly. Ringle is undoubtedly faster than Surprise, but I would not have her passengers unduly cramped — given a disgust of the sea — for the sake of a few days.'

'Two ladies, one gentleman, three children, and I suppose three or four maids and a man.'

'It does of course depend upon whether the gentleman chooses to come.' observed Jack 'Mr Harding, you will read the letters: they are not in any way confidential.'

'I make no doubt that the gentleman will come.' said Stephen.

Harding, a posed middle-aged man, read the letters with attention. The others watched him. 'Well, sir,' he said at last 'Well, gentlemen: I am of opinion that Ringle is the right choice. I were perpetually easy of my sheet when in company with Surprise, though indeed there are few faster frigates. They will not be at their ease to be sure, but they will have the delight of the bow-wave flung out to leeward & the wake racing away everything alive & tearing through the water. They would be dull souls as did not love that: and if I may be so bold Miss Bridget loved it pretty last time she were afloat in a blow. Anyhow you would want Ringle as a tender, sir.'

'Very true: so you think all those people could be crammed in?.'

'I should take my davy on it, sir.'

'Very well. You can set sail with Surprise, then; and she will deliver my officers passengers & dispatches at Portsmouth, then if run down to be laid up in Seppings's yard.'

'Very good, sir,' said Harding, folding the letters away in his bosom. 'So now, since the gentlemen for Portsmouth are already aboard *Surprise*, I shall ask permission to take my leave and wish you and *Suffolk* a happy, prosperous voyage. And Doctor, how I hope you and your mate may bag a brace or two of phoenixes.'

They shook hands and parted. 'There is a fine fellow,' said Jack. 'He can sail the schooner very, very hard indeed: it was the right choice. But I think he was not mistaken when he said they would not always lie at their ease.'

'It would be ill-natured on my part to suggest that he might be influenced by the certainty, under Providence, of coming back to your blue squadron and acting as tender to the imposing great *Suffolk* under your command: I shall not say it however, although my lower being does feel exceptionally bad-tempered today. Jack, with your idea you have wholly forestalled me. You spoke of a notion worthy of Newton, but you did not elaborate: and I was only waiting for an opportunity of telling you mine.'

'Pray do so now, dear Stephen: I am sure it would be more luminous.'

'What I was going to say was that you had no idea of the fundamental difference between a mere landlubber and a seaman.'

'Oh was you, indeed?'

'You may toss your head in that superior way, but you have never been a *mere* landlubber. You were introduced to the ocean as an infant child; you boated before you knew the difference between right and wrong; you went positively to sea under Captain Willis well before puberty. Far from you the wondering calf-like gaze of those who watch the intrepid mariner traverse the tossing deck – the gaze almost instantly followed by a feeling of unavoidable and certain death, cold death, followed by furious uncontrollable heaves and

'Very good, sir.' said Harding, folding the letters away in his bosom. 'So now, since the gentlemen to be carried to Portsmouth are already aboard Surprise, I shall ask your permission to take my leave and wish you a Suffolk & happy, prosperous voyage. And Doctor, how I hope you both & your mate will bag a brace or two of phoenixes.'

They shook hands and parted. 'There is a fine fellow.' said Jack. 'He can sail the schooner very, very hard indeed: it was the right choice. But I think he was right when he said they would not always lie at their ease.'

'It would be ill-natured on my part to suggest that he might be influenced by the certainty, under Providence, of coming back to your blue squadron and acting as tender to the imposing great Suffolk under your command: I shall not say it however, although my lower nature does feel exceptionally ill-tempered today. Jack, with your idea you have wholly forestalled me. You spoke of a notion worthy of Newton, but you did not elaborate: and I was only waiting for an opportunity of telling you mine.'

'Pray do so now, dear Stephen: I am sure it would be more luminous.'

'What I was going to say was that you had no idea of the fundamental difference between a landlubber and a seaman.'

'Oh, was you, indeed?'

'You may toss your head in the superior way, but you have never been a mere landlubber. You were introduced to the ocean as an infant child; you boated before you knew the difference between right and wrong; you went positively to sea under Captain Willis well before puberty. Far from you the wondering calf-life gaze of those that watch the tortured mariner traverse the tossing deck — the gaze almost instantly followed by the feeling of unavoidable & certain death, cold death. followed by furious uncontrollable heaves and

shameless vomiting, morbid frigor and despair. They, with some slight recovery and even an upright position, the sight of these god-like creatures stalking about the nightmare deck in their uncouth garments, uttering their brutish cries, haling upon ropes great and small – finding their way by night – reaching the stated port – all this reduces the lubber to a state of laudable and permanent humility. No, no, my good sir, you may say what you please, but there is a great gulf fixed between the landlubber – the landlubber who comes late to things that float – and the true-born seaman: a gulf as great as that between a sheep and a seal.'

'Very true,' said Jack, who had had the training of some of the sheep.

'Now you are to consider,' Stephen went on, 'that my Brigid was not only baptized in sea-water, but dipped before she could walk. When we were ashore she rejoiced in boats, when we were afloat she delighted in heavy sea, never minding in the least when they soaked her through and through – nimble in the rigging, the darling of the upper-yardmen. She often explains the rigging to me, and I have seen old hands like Tobin nod with approval. No, my dear Jack, what I should have said had you not in essence said it before me, was that one (however young) who has sea-legs, sea-sense and a knowledge both acquired and to some degree as it were instinctive of the sea's very nature itself bears down all frippery land-based experience, however old.'

'Oh come, Stephen, Charlotte and what's her name are not exactly crones. As I remember they only date from the Mauritius campaign.'

'They might have been born with Helen of Troy as far as that is concerned. Aboard, particularly aboard so lithe and eager a vessel as *Ringle*, Brigid must bear them down; and a just equilibrium will be reached, with mutual respect and no bullying.'

THERE WERE MANY vantage-points high above the harbour that

starve starving

shameless vomiting, morbid frigor and despair. Then, with some slight recovery and even an inveigned position. the sight of these god-like creatures walking the nightmare deck in these uncouth garments, uttering these brutish cries, hauling upon ropes great & small — finding their way by night — reaching the slide port! — No, no, my good sir, you may say what you like, but there is a great gulf fixed between the land-lubber — the land-lubber who comes late to things that float — and the true born seaman; a gulf as as great as that between a sheep and a seal.

'Very true,' said Jack, who had heard the braying of some of the sheep.

'Now you are to consider,' Stephen went on, 'that my Bridget was not only baptized in sea-water, but dipped before she could walk. When we were ashore she rejoiced in boats, when we were at sea-sh afloat she delighted in heavy seas, never minding in the least when they soaked her through and through — nimble in the rigging, the darling of the upper yardmen. She often explains the rigging to me, & and I have seen wise old hands like Tobin nod with approval. No, my dear Jack, what I should have said had you not in essence said it before me, was that one (however young) who has sea-legs, sea-sense, and a knowledge both acquired & to some degree as it were instinctive of the sea's very nature itself, bears down all frippery land-based experience, however old.'

'Oh come, Stephen: Charlotte & what's her name are not exactly cloners. As I remember they only date from the Mauritius camp campaign.'

'They might have been born with Helen of Troy as far as that is concerned. Aboard, particularly aboard so lithe and eager a vessel as Ringle, she must bear them down: and a just equilibrium with be reached, with mutual respect & no bullying.

Bridget

There were many vantage points about the harbour that

Jack and Stephen used to climb, once a reasonable period had elapsed, a period in which a well-handled weatherly craft with favourable winds (and as far as could be told they had been favourable) could reasonably be expected to sail out and back; and Stephen had the pleasure of seeing some moderately upland birds and the bizarre mating habits of a colony of variegated scorpions, while the sun passed over the almost invariable translucent sky; but Jack always made his descent to the still fairly active yards (Lord Leyton's mainmast footing still gave great trouble) with hope disappointed.

By now *Suffolk* was in very fine fig, and since Jack was blessed with an experienced and upon the whole intelligent wardroom, the gun-crews, at least in dumb-show, were as brisk as he could wish while the small-arms men (who could, within limits, fire their pieces) were all well above the average. Her stores were completed – prime salt beef from the immense ranches, smaller amounts of moderate pork, a remarkably agreeable army biscuit, tobacco in industrial quantities – while for daily use flesh-boats plied to and from the butchers stalls along the quay, and flat-bottomed craft brought fruit and vegetables in unlimited amount. As a peace-maker the Nuncio had worked wonders, though to be sure commercial enterprise had played its part.

'It is only a Friday,' said Jack, when he and his first lieutenant (he sailed without a flag-captain) had made sure that there was not a becket out of place and that all Suffolks were present, correctly shaved and provided with all that was required. 'It is only a Friday, but I think I shall stroll up well beyond our usual mound with a telescope. Do you choose to come, Stephen?'

'I do, too: we might see some of the first migrants.'

Up and up: fairly easy going now that they were used to the land; and as they rose the horizon increased enormously, the empty horizon, though in with the land there were some lateen-rigged fishermen.

The mound they chose was thinly covered with a sparse herbage in which there grew a small particularly vicious cactus, while in the many bare places the earth showed

Jack & Stephen climbed once: a fairly seasonable time had elapsed,
and Stephen had at least the delight of some ~~reasonably~~ moderately upland birds
and the bizarre mating habits of a colony of variegated scorpions while
the sun passed over the almost invariably pure translucent sky; but
Jack made his descent to the still fairly active yards (Lord L's
ship was in the last stages of painting) with hope disappointed.

Suffolk by now was ∅ in very fine fog, and since Jack
was blessed with an experienced, ~~extell~~ and upon the whole
intelligent wardroom, the gun-crews, at least in dumb-show,
were as brisk as he could wish. While the small-arms men
(who could, within limits, fire their pieces) ~~& were~~ were well above
the average. His stores were of course completed – ~~free~~ prime salt
beef from the immense tanches, water straight from ~~the~~ conduits fed in
the mountain, an ~~eminently~~ remarkably agreeable ~~portable~~ army biscuit – while for everyday
use the flesh-boat plied to and fro, while flat-bottomed craft brought
stout and vegetables in unbounded quantity ~~from the butchers'~~ stalls along the quay.
As a peace-maker the Nuncio had worked wonders. though to be sure, commercial
eagerness had its share

'It is only a Friday,' said Jack. when he and his first lieutenant
(he ~~said~~ sailed without a flag-captain) had made sure that there was not
a becket out of place and that all Suffolks were present. correctly shaved
and provided with all that was required. 'It is only a Friday.
but I think I shall stroll up beyond our usual mound with a
telescope. Do you choose to come?'

'I do too: we might see some of the first migrants.'

Up and up: fairly easy going now that they were used to it
land; and as they rose the horizon increased enoro enormously,
the empty horizon. though in ~~with~~ to land there were some ~~fish~~
fishermen - lateen-rigged.

The mound on which they sat was thinly ~~cauliousth~~ covered with a
sparse herbage. ~~but~~ in the many bare places the earth showed

ultimate

raller
shits of
stale pork

old as pluton
1 3rd 99

on which there grew.
small particularly reven cactus

dull purplish red: a landscape more wholly foreign they had never seen, although they had travelled very, very widely – it was, after all, their calling.

'Dear Lord,' said Jack, sitting comfortably down, his back to a rock, after a piercing search of the nearer sea and the northern horizon, 'how I long for Woolcombe and the green Woolhampton downs, speckled with sheep. Woolcombe and the soft dew falling: the cawing of rooks. When I was a mere post-captain, you know, and there was this prospect of peace, I used to console myself, particularly when I was solvent again with that dear prize-money and Cousin Edward's land doing so well – I used to console myself with the thought of restoring the place to what it was when I was a boy, before my father lost his head about the Stock Exchange, when we had a pack of hounds and a damned good huntsman and when the water-bailiff kept the streams as neat as a man-of-war: full of trout and the odd salmon on the spring run. Lord, we had such sport, such fun! There was an old hound called Captain, and he always hit off the line after a check. "Hark to Captain" we would cry, and they all followed him like a single creature. Lord! How I longed to be back! Now of course I must stand my trick as a flag-officer: and most uncommon lucky I am to *have* it to do. But I do so long to be back, sometimes, under Hamble Down, showing George how to work out a line. Stephen, you can have no idea how beautiful it is.'

'Can I not?'

'Oh of course you can, of course you can. I am sure the Glens of Avoca are even finer. I do beg your pardon. But, do you see, it was *my* childhood.'

'Have you noticed that small vessel right in with the land, almost beneath us, under the cliff? Her sails are all in a line.'

Jack leapt to his feet. 'By God, she's *Ringle*,' he cried. 'She must have stood inshore . . .' The voice and the explanation died on the downward slope.

'I should never have believed

dull purplish red: a landscape as ~~utterly~~ wholly foreign than had ever seen. although they had travelled not indeed from port to port but very, very widely — it was after all their calling.

'Dear Lord.' said Jack after a piercing search of the inshore sea and the northern horizon, 'how I long for Woolcombe. and the ~~soft~~ green Woolhampton Downs. speckled with sheep. Woolcombe's and the soft rain falling. When I was a mere post-captain. you know, and there was this prospect of peace. I used to console myself. particularly when I was solvent again with that dear prize-money and Cousin Edward's land doing so well. I used to console myself with the thought of restoring the place to what it was when I was a boy. before my father lost his head about the Stock Exchange when we had a pack of hounds and a damned good huntsman, and the water-bailiff kept the streams as trim as a man-of-war: full of trout. and the odd salmon in the spring run. Lord. we had such sport. such fun! There was an old hound called Captain. and he always hit the line ~~off~~ after a check — they followed him like an oracle. Lord. how I longed to be back! Now of course I have to serve my trick as a flag-officer: ~~a~~ most uncommon lucky I am to have it to do. But how I long to be back. sometimes. under Hampshire Downs. showing George how to work out a line. Stephen. you can have no idea how beautiful it is.'

'Can I not?.'

I am sure the Glories of Avoca are even finer

'Oh. of course you can. of course you can. I beg your pardon.'
do

'Have you noticed that small vessel right in under the land. almost beneath us. under the cliff?'. Her sails all in. low

Jack leapt to his feet. 'By God. she's Ringle.' he cried. 'She must have stood inshore' Her voice and his explanation died on the downward. 'I should never have

Beloved

that a man so tall and stout could have moved so fast,' murmured Stephen, fixing the schooner in his glass. He liked to believe that he could make out Brigid and Christine with Edward Heatherleigh clinging to a spar behind them, but it was clearly time to descend.

The perilous slope, the milder slope, the mule-track, the paved road, and at last the quays with Jack still far, far ahead, though now moving more like an admiral.

Ringle was a beautifully-proportioned vessel and it was only when there was a tight knot of people on her fo'c'sle that one saw how small she was in fact. Kindly hands heaved on the mooring ropes to let Stephen step aboard from the quay, and clear over the general din he heard the Aubrey twins' shrill cry, raised for the seventh time, 'Why are you not wearing your admiral's uniform?' while at the same time his own Brigid slipped through the throng and whispered 'Dearest Papa' as he bent to kiss her. Christine was just behind, and looking up from the child's shining, happy, sun-browned face he said, 'Dear Christine, she does you infinite credit. Edward, my dear sir, how do you do? How happy I am to see you.'

The visitors' cabins had long since been prepared, and now the admiral's barge car-ried them over: after their extraordinarily rapid but somewhat cramped voyage they were amazed by the scale of a ship of the line. 'It is almost as good as Grignon's hotel,' said Charlotte, which earned her a sour look from Killick. 'And have you noticed that the sails are square?' asked her sister, to which Brigid replied, 'Don't you know the odds between a ship and a schooner?' with such firmness and such effect that Stephen saw, with infinite satisfaction, that a decent balance had been established. Then again, Brigid knew quantities of old Surprises, some of whom had taught her the ropes: these she found out and asked them how they did, calling them by name,

that a tall man so stout could have moved so fast,' said Stephen, fixing the schooner with his glass. He longed to believe that he could make out Christine and Brigid with Edward Heatherleigh clinging to a spar behind them, but it was clearly time to descend. ⑤

The perilous slope, the milder slope, the mule-track, the paved road and at last the Quays with [faces] still far ahead, but moving ever more [vitro] are admired.

It was Ringle was a beautifully proportioned vessel and it was only when there was a tight knot of people on her fo'c'sle that one saw how small she was in fact. Kindly hands heaved in mooring ropes to let Stephen step aboard from the quay and close over the general din he heard the Aubrey twins' shrill cry raised for the seventh time 'Why are you not wearing your uniform?', while at the same time his own Brigid slipped through the throng and whispered 'Dearest Papa,' as he bent to kiss her. Christine was fast behind her, and looking at her from a childish, sunburnt face he said 'Dear Christine. She deserves you infinite credit. Edward, my dear sir, how do you do?'.

The visitors' cabins had long since been prepared, and now the admirable barge carried them over: # after a somewhat cramped but phenomenally rapid voyage they were amazed by the scale of a ship of the time. 'It is almost as good as Gregoire's hotel,' said Charlotte, which brought her a cross look from Killick. And 'Have you noticed that the sails are square?' asked her sister, to which Brigid answered replied 'Don't you know the difference between a ship and a schooner?' with such firmness, and to such effect that Stephen saw, with infinite satisfaction, that his theory had not been mistaken, that a decent balance had been restored.⊕ And not only that, but Brigid knew quantities of old Surprises,* found them out and asked them how they did, calling them by name.

* some of whom had taught her the ropes,

which put her head and shoulders above any passenger but Mrs Aubrey. In any case the twins never entered into competition: as might have been predicted, they had been dreadfully seasick, confined to their bunks, horrible to see and worse to hear from the very beginning until a few days ago, so that they had acquired no sea-legs, no fundamental knowledge; and even now they were incapable of distinguishing a bowline from a rolling-hitch.

Yet in a surprisingly short time as it is measured by days the new inhabitants of the *Suffolk*, even the more stupid of the Aubrey girls, took bells for granted, the ritual swabbing of decks, set meals (less Spartan now that they lay in port) and the many and very fine gradations that separated the rear-admiral from the boy, third-class. Stephen observed, with a mute but intense satisfaction, that here his daughter had not the least air of being a stranger in the house, a friend's child accepted for that friend's sake: here, with so many friends and accompanied by Padeen, an old Surprise of remarkable standing and authority, she was very much at home. Yet as far as he could see she did not flaunt her sea-going knowledge, but as soon as the twins were willing to be peaceable she was both kind and companion-like.

Very soon they had explored almost every part of the ship from the safer tops (propelled by Padeen and other seamen) to the echoing vaults of the darkened hold, where facetious midshipmen and first class volunteers would terrify them with sepulchral moans and waving sheets.

'Dearest Stephen,' said Sophie, passing him a cup of tea in the cabin, 'I cannot tell you how glad I am that our daughters are friends again: there was a time when I almost despaired – when I should have whipped them if I had not thought

86

which put her head and shoulders above any passenger but Mrs Aubrey.

✱ [to bottom p 7] Furthermore the twins, as might have been predicted, had been dreadfully seasick, confined to their bunks, horrible to see & worse to hear, from the very beginning until a few days ago, so that they had acquired no sea-legs, no fundamental knowledge, so that even now they were & incapable of distinguishing between a rolling-hitch and a bowline.

In e surprisingly short time as it is measured by days the new inhabitants of the Suffolk, particularly the children, took both for granted, the relieve's swallowing of decks, set meals (as Spartan now that they lay in port), the many & very fine gradations that separated the rear-admiral from the boy, third class. Stephen observed, with a small but intense satisfaction, that here his daughter, ~~though supported of & could~~ by Padeen, an old Sophron of ~~remarkable standing and authority~~ had not the least air of being a stranger in his house, a friend's child accepted for that friend's sake: here, with so many friends and accompanied by Padeen, an old Sophron of remarkable standing & authority, ~~and compared with such a friend of George's~~ knowledge she was very much at home. Yet as far as he could see she did not flaunt her sea-going knowledge. But as soon as the twins were willing to be peaceable she was both kind and & companionable

Very soon they had explored almost every part of the ship, from the safer tops (propelled Padeen & other seamen) to the echoing vaults of the darkened hold where facetious midshipmen any first class volunteers would terrify them with sepulchral moans & wavy sheets.

'Dearest Stephen, said Sophie, passing him a cup of tea in the cabin. 'I cannot tell you how glad I am that our daughters are friends again: there was a time yr at home when I almost despaired - when I should have whipped them if I had not thought

it would do more harm than good. It only made me dogged when I was young.'

'I cannot imagine you being whipped, Sophie,' said Christine.

'But I was, and quite often too. My mother would make us stand with our faces to the wall and whip the back of our legs with a thin sheaf of willow-wands: I do not think it ever improved my French verbs or arithmetic or even my manners.'

'I knew some Dominican nuns who did that,' said Stephen. 'They whipped my Saavedra cousins until they bled: I had thought it was only Catholic. Jack hardly ever flogs: discourages it, indeed. How do you find him, my dear?'

'Oh, very well, I thank you,' said Sophie, blushing. 'I must admit he is rather thinner than I could wish: but he does *love* having his flag, and I am so very, very happy for him. It was Prince William who sent us the news, with his best compliments, which I thought wonderfully polite.'

The three little girls came in, since if there was tea there might also, in the nature of things, be cake, or at least muffin. On seeing Stephen they stopped, not looking very wise, and made a concerted bob: then Brigid ran over to him and said, 'Oh sir, the Admiral says a Portuguee came in with the flood and he hopes there may be some mail. A boat pulled across to the flag not long since.'

'I shall go upstairs – I shall go on deck, and ask whether it would be proper to enquire. Ladies, forgive me, I beg.'

No. It would be most improper. Jack was surprised that a man who had seen so much sea-time could suppose the thing possible or even decent – it was not exactly mutinous but it would deserve and certainly receive an exceptionally harsh reproach. But in any case Stephen was talking great nonsense. The Portuguese had been aboard Lord Leyton this hour and more and there

it would do more harm than good. It only made me dogged when I
was young.'

'I cannot imagine you being whipped, Sophie,' said Christine.

'But I so was, and quite often too. My mother would make us
stand with our faces to the wall and whip the back of our legs
with a scourge made of willow-wands. I do not think it ever
improved my French verbs or arithmetic or even my manners.'

'I knew some Dominican nuns who did that,' said Stephen.
'They whipped my Saavedra cousins until they bled: I had supposed
it was only Catholic. Jack hardly ever flogs: discourages it, indeed.
How do you find him, my dear?'

'Oh, very well, I thank you,' said Sophie, blushing. 'I must
admit he is rather sterner than I could wish: but he does look
harassed less flag, and I am so very very happy for him. It
was Prince William who sent us the news, with his best compliments
which I thought was wonderfully polite.'

The three little girls came in, since if there were their there
might also, in the nature of things, be cake, or at least muffin. On
seeing Stephen they stopped, not looking very wise, and curtseyed and
made a concerted bob; then Brigid ran over to him and said Oh
sir, the Admiral says a Portugee came in with the flood and
he hopes there may be some mail. A boat pulled across to
the flagg' not long since.'

'I shall go upstairs – I shall go on deck, and ask whether
it would be proper to enquire. Ladies, forgive me, I beg.'

No. It would be most improper. Jack was surprised that
a man who had seen so much sea-time could suppose such a
thing possible or even decent – it was not exactly mutinous but
it would deserve and most receive an exceedingly bitter reproach.
But in any case Stephen was talking great nonsense. The Portuguese
had been aboard Lord Leyton this hour and more and then

had been no sign of mail – nothing handed up the side, no passing out of bags, no hurrying to and fro. No. The boat had done nothing more than deliver a gentleman, the gentleman in regimentals who was now walking up and down the quarterdeck with the Admiral, arm in arm. 'I have been staring at him with my glass, in this ill-bred fashion, for some little time,' said Jack. 'For although I think I know the face and carriage I cannot put a name to either. Should you like to take a look?'

'Sure, it is very ill-bred: but I might, to make you easy.' Stephen took the telescope, focused it, and almost at once, as the two men on the far ship turned, he said coldly, 'It is Henry Miller. He was at Trinity in my time and he killed Edward Taaffe in the Fifteen Acres when I was in my last year.'

'Miller? Yes, of course, my neighbour over by Caxley. He must be related to the Admiral – Miller is Lord Leyton's family name, and that person over there often spoke of a peerage going to some fairly close connexion. Cousin, of course: they would not be walking arm in arm, otherwise.' After a pause Jack went on, 'What do you mean by your Fifteen Acres?'

'It is a space in the Phoenix Park – you know the great park in Dublin, I am sure?' Jack nodded. 'And that is where people go, particularly the young men of Trinity, to settle matters of honour.'

'Just so: and he killed a gunner officer in Malta, too. He is said to be a very good shot; and he has capital pistols. I have heard him called Hair-Trigger Miller; and to be sure I have seen him bring down a great many pheasants.'

'Would you say he was a quarrelsome man, at all?'

'I scarcely know him. We are necessarily acquainted, but he is not the sort of man whose acquaintance I should value – in short, I do not like him. It is not the fighting. As you know, duels are much more usual in the army than with us, or even the Marines. And anyhow you and I have both been out from time to time . . . cannot top it the Holy Joe.'

nothing carried up the side,

is no sign of mail — /no handing out of bags, no hurrying to and
fro. No. The boat had done nothing more than deliver the gentleman
the gentleman in regimentals who is walking up and down the quarterdeck
with the Admiral arm in arm. I have been staring at him with my
glass in this ill-bred fashion for some little time. for although I think
I know the face I cannot put a name to it. Will you take a look?'

'Sure it's very ill-bred: but I might, to make you easy.' He
took the telescope, focus focussed, and almost at once, as the wind
blew on the far ship turned, he said coldly. 'It is Henry Miller.
He was at Trinity and he killed Edward Taaffe on the Fifteen Acres when
I was in my last year.'

'Miller? Yes: that is Lord Leyton's family name. They meant to
Yes, of course, my neighbours over by Caxley: he must be related
to the Admiral — Miller is Lord Leyton's family name. and the man
I know often spoke of a peerage given to some fairly close connexion
cousin. of course they would not be walking arm in arm, else.'
After a pause Jack went on. 'He killed a gunner-major in Malta
too. He is said — obviously, to be a very good shot, with. captain
for pistol: I have heard him called Trav. Trigger Miller, and to be
sure I have seen him bring down a great many pheasants.'

'Would you say he was a quarrelsome man at all?'

'I scarcely know him. We are unresearch acquainted, but I do
he is not the kind of man whose acquaintance I should value.
in short I do not like him. It is not his fighting. Duels are
much more usual in the army than with us, as you know: and
anyhow we have both them out from time to time....'

(— 39)

Jack stared out over the water and went on. 'For all I know he may be well enough liked in his regiment: but his reputation in the neighbourhood is so indifferent that I was astonished to learn that he had called on Edward and Christine when they settled in Medenham, and then at Woolcombe when Christine was staying there, with Edward so far in the north. I have no room to blackguard a man for incontinence, being no model myself: but there are limits . . . You know very well, Stephen, how much influence a man with a large household and a considerable estate can bring to bear on his dependents – his dependents' daughters – and there were some very ugly tales of girls in child being turned away. I *know* very little: yet his conduct does seem to match with the general reprobation.'

'He is not married, I take it?'

'No, nor ever has been. Being almost next in succession to the Leyton title, he is said to be saving himself up for some very brilliant match.'

'Can you square a man's valuing a peerage very highly with his going out and risking his life so often?'

'Yes, if he is an unusually resentful unloved creature and at the same time an uncommon good shot.'

'Sir, if you please,' said the officer of the watch, stepping aft and taking off his hat, 'Flag is breaking out a signal.' Speaking in the high, staccato, expressionless voice usual on such occasions, the duty-midshipman piped up, 'Flag to *Suffolk*: Admiral invites Rear-Admiral and Doctor M-A-T-U-R-I-N to dinner at a quarter past three: repeat a quarter past three o'clock.'

'Rear-Admiral to flag: very happy,' said Jack in italics. Then he hurried aft to Stephen's point of discreet withdrawal. 'Stephen, I have engaged you to dine with the Admiral tomorrow: I hope you do not mind it?'

'I do not mind it, my dear: and it would make not odds if I did. We are all worms under the harrow, in the service: even you,

Jack stared over the water and went on.

'For all I know he may very well be well enough liked in his regiment. but his reputation in the neighbourhood is so indifferent that I was surprised to learn that he had called on Edward and Christine when they settled in Medenham. and then at Woolcoat when Christine was staying there with to Edward so busy in the north. I have no room to blackguard, man for incontinence. being no model myself; but there are bounds... You know very well, Stephen, how much influence a of man with a large household and a considerable estate can bring to bear on his dependants — his dependents' daughters — and there were some very ugly tales of girls in child being turned away.' 'I know very little. Yet his conduct. does seem to match with the general reprobation.'

'He is not married. I take it?.'

'No. Not ever has been. Since he is next in succession to Leyta title, he is said to be saving himself up for some very brilliant match.'

'Can you square a man's valuing a peerage very highly with his going out and risking his life so often?.'

'Yes. if he is an unusually resentful creature and at the same time a very good shot.'
^{unloved}

'Sir, if you please.' said the officer of the watch, stepping aft and taking off his hat. 'Flag is breaking out a signal.'

Speaking in the high. staccato. expressionless voice usual on such occasions midshipman piped up 'Flag to Suffolk: Admiral invites Rear-Admiral and Doctor MATURIN, to dinner at a quarter past three, repeat a quarter past three.'
^{spell out}

'Rear. Admiral to flag: very happy,' said Jack in stilted & then. speaking more like a human being. 'Pass the word for the Doctor.. Stephen, (in a proud low, and then leaning over the taffrail) I have engaged you to dine with the Admiral tomorrow: I hope you do not mind it?.'

'I do not mind it. my dear; and it would make no odds if I did. We are all worms under the harrow, in the service. even you.

Weber's clarinet concerto n(?)A perhaps rather wordy but most agreeable

Jack, scintillating in gold lace, are but one of us. *I say come, and he cometh: for I am a centurion*. I have met few admirals: some high, mighty and almost certainly constipated; others small, jolly, good company: reading men, even. Besides, I long for men's company: the prattle of the little girls – much though I love them – drives me to an earlier and earlier breakfast, to a later and even later dinner, so that presently the two will meet, as they did in Avicenna's tale. They come to me with a pelagic crab, a starfish, a piece of common wrack, and standing by my side they cry, "Oh sir, pray tell us what it is," so that I am tempted to utter obscene blasphemy. Oh how I long for dear Jacob's return!'

'I believe our departure depends largely on that,' said Jack gravely; and then after a pause, 'I tell you what, Stephen,' he cried, 'it is long since we had a real great-gun exercise. The last powder-hoy, for a trifle of whiskey – you know the Irish drink, Stephen, I am sure?'

'I have never heard of it,' said Stephen.

'– gave us a little surplus, so that the gunner is actually at a loss to stow it: nothing could be happier. And if that does not deafen, astound and silence the little girls there is the Devil in it. I shall give orders directly. The whole *shooting-match!*" Jack did not often stumble on a witticism, and this one gave him particular delight: he repeated it twice.

The whole shooting-match it was, indeed: *Suffolk* might not have been called a very taut ship, nor more than ordinarily crack, but she could never have been likened to the Margate hoy; and in any case she now carried many Surprises, long used to their captain's ways and his rigid insistence upon very high

Jack, fairly scintillating in gold lace, are but one of us. I say come, and he cometh. for I am a centurion. But in any case, I should like to meet this admiral. I have met few: some high-mighty, and almost certainly constipated, others small, jolly, and good company. Reading men, even. Besides, I long for men's company: the prattle of the little girls — much though I love them — drives me to an earlier and earlier breakfast, & a later and even later dinner, so that presently the two will meet, as they did in Avicenna's tale. They come to me with a pelagic crab, a starfish, a piece of common wrack, and standing by my side they cry 'Oh sir, pray tell me what it is,' so that I am tempted to utter obscene blasphemy. Oh how I long for dear Jacob's return!.

'I believe our departure depends largely on that,' said Jack gravely; and then he paused. 'I tell you what, Stephen,' he cried. 'It is long since we had a real great-gun exercise. The last hoy = for a trifle of whiskey — you know the touch down, Stephen, I am sure?'.

'I have never heard of it,' said Stephen.

'— gave us a little surplus, so that the gunner is actually [41] at a loss how to stow it: nothing could be happier. And if that does not deafen, astound and silence the little girls there is the Devil in it, I shall give orders directly. The whole shooting-match!' — Jack did not often stumble on a witticism, and this one gave him particular delight.

The whole shooting match it were, indeed: Suffolk might not have been called a very taut ship, or more than ordinarily crack, but it could never have been likened to a Margate hoy, and in any up case it now carried many Surprises, long used to their captain's ways, and his rigid insistence upon a very high

standards indeed. The breeze being both steady and favourable Jack laid on his favourite, most profitable form of exercise, one calculated to promote zeal, speed and above all accuracy, to knit a gun-crew into an immensely cooperative whole – never a word passing, never a word called for – and to promote the most valuable sort of competition. The most experienced gun-captains and the older, wiser midshipmen were at the three forward guns; and bitter shame would fall upon any following gun that could not keep up with them in speed or accuracy.

The first three guns had been ordered to fire high, to leave something for the rest of the broadside; and Jack, as a particular treat, silencer or gob-stopper for the little girls, had with Mr Meares the gunner contrived a flimsy but coherent structure that under very light and worn-out canvas would drift until it was abreast of the man-of-war, which would then pound it with the most rapid broadside compatible with the *Suffolk's* timbers – a broadside rolling, but only just rolling.

'Target's away,' hailed the foretopmast lookout. 'On deck, there, target's away.'

'From forward aft as she bears,' called Jack; and there was a long, tense silence, broken only by the gentle wind in the rigging. The little girls, in white frocks, stood on tip-toe: just behind them Sophie and Christine, almost equally tense. The captain of Number One glared along his sights, the lanyard in his right hand, his left making very slight delicate motions to swivel or elevate the huge gun-barrel right or left, up or down a trifle. 'Fire!' he cried and heaved on the lanyard: the hammer shot forward and with barely a perceptible pause the gun uttered its prodigious roar, a great jet of smoke and flame enveloping the cannon-ball and the gun-carriage and cannon raced inboard with a screech of trunions under the arched bodies of the crew until the whole was brought up short with a great twang

standards indeed. The breeze being both steady and favourable Jack had laid on his favourite, most profitable form of exercise, one calculated to promote zeal, speed, & above all accuracy, to unite a gun-crew into an immensely active cooperation while — never a word passing, never a word called for — and to promote the most valuable sort of competition. The most experienced gun-captains and the older, more midshipmen were at the three forward guns; and bitter shame would fall upon any following gun that could not keep up with them in speed or accuracy.

The first three guns had been ordered to fire high, to leave sensible for the rest of the broadside; and Jack, as a particular treat silencer or gob-stopper for the wells girls, had, with the gunner, Mr Mason, contrived a flimsy but coherent structure that could, very light and worn out canvas, would drift slowly until it was abreast of the man-of-war, which would then pound it with the most rapid broadside compatible with Sophie's timbers — rolling, but only just rolling.

'Target's away,' hailed the forecastle lookout. 'On deck there. Target's away.'

'From forward aft she bears,' called Jack, and there was a long, tense silence, broken only by the gentle wind in the rigging. The little girls, in volute frocks, stood a-tip-toe: just behind them Sophie and Christine, almost equally tense. The captain of Number One glared along his sights... the lanyard in his right hand, his left making very slight delicate movements to swivel or elevate the long gun-barrel right or left, up or down a little. 'Fire!' he cried and heaved on the lanyard: the hammer shot forward and with barely the least perceptible pause the gun uttered its prodigious roar. a great jet of smoke and flame enveloping the cannon ball and the racing gun-carriage and barrel racing inboard with a screech of trucks under the arched bodies of its crew until the whole was brought up short with a great twang

of the tackles; but already there were immensely active hands cleaning any smouldering remnants from the gun, swabbing the barrel, ramming down the next charge of powder, then the ball, then the wads, well thumped down, the crew barely pausing for breath but running the whole mass up against the side with a crash, where the gun-captain pricked and primed his cock, unmoved by the truly appalling discharge of his right-hand neighbour as he and his mates made all fast and levelled the warm gun again.

The firing went clean down the battleship's side at a fine even pace, and even the aftermost piece had its shot at the frail remnant that drifted by. But by then the little girls had almost no voice to screech with nor even the emotional power to do so: the enormous and repeated din, the vibration of the ship and the air, the great flashes and the dense clouds of smoke drifting away to leeward had overpowered them; and the near-stupefaction of their elders was very impressive too. Sophie had seen sloops and moderate frigates at gun-exercise, but never a ship of the line, and she was quite remarkably perturbed, not only by the unconscionable din but infinitely more by the reflection that this was what his profession inflicted upon her husband: or at least the way of life to which it exposed him. Christine, to to be sure, had fired many and many a fowling-piece and even upon occasion a rifled gun, but nothing imaginably on this scale, and she remained quite mute, holding Brigid's hand, until after a good deal of calling-out right forward the cry came down, 'On deck, on deck there. Target's away, sir.'

So it was, a great long affair of all kinds of old casks and nameless objects from the entire squadron clapped together and furnished with enough cloth of a sort to carry the whole downwind. The target appeared on the starboard bow, towed by boats that cast off as soon as it was well on course. An active intelligent master's mate ran down the broadside: 'No fire until the Admiral gives the word: then count

by the tackles: but already there were immensely active hands clearing any smouldering remnants from the gun, swabbing the barrel, ramming down the next charge of powder, the wad, then the ward, well thumped down, and barely pausing for the breech running the whole mass not up against the side, at which the captain pointed and primed her cock, unmoved by the truly appalling of his neighbour as he and his mates made all fast and levelled the warm gun again.

The firing went clear down the battleship's side at a few time even pace, and even the sternmost piece had its shot at the frail remnant that drifted by. But by this the little girls had almost no voice to screech nor even the emotional power to do so: the enormous and repeated din, the vibration of the ship and the air, the great flashes and the dense cloud of smoke drifting away to leeward had overpowered them; and the near-stupefaction of their elders was very impressive too. Sophie had seen sloops & moderate frigates at gun-exercise, but never a ship of the line, and she was much remarkably perturbed, not only by the unconscionable din but intimately more than by the reflection that this was what his profession subject her husband to. Christine, to be sure, had fired many and many a fowling-piece and even a rifled gun on occasion, but nothing imaginably on this scale, and she yet remained quite mute, holding Brigid's hand, until after a good deal of calling out right forward the cry came down. 'On deck, on deck there. Target's away, sir.'

So it was, a great long ramshackle affair of all kinds of old casks and nameless objects, clapped together and furnished with every cloth of a sort to carry it whole downwind. The target appeared on the starboard bow, loosed too by boats their cast off as soon as it was well on. An active intelligent master's mate ran down the broadside 'No fire until the Admiral gives the word: then count

11.8

two between each shot.'

A profound silence: the target drifted half way down the *Suffolk*'s length. 'Fire,' said Jack.

The first gun and before it quite ran in the second and so clear along down to the last: and when the smoke cleared and the last repeated echo died away there was nothing but tossing water to be seen. The little girls had strength enough to utter a last gasping 'Oh,' and then they were led away, exhausted: but not before a furious Killick had appeared on the quarterdeck waving a full-dress coat. 'Which I had it all laid out a quarter of an hour long past. Ain't you got . . .' He was going to say 'no shame?' but disapproving looks, coupled with Jack's compliance and a call for the barge checked his zeal.

With a following breeze and a very well-inclined crew the barge fairly skimmed across the sea, hooking on only a matter of seconds late. In any case Lord Leyton was in a good mood – he could be jovial and he could be damned crabbed: but this was a good day. He had heard much of Dr Maturin's acquaintance, close acquaintance, with Prince William, who, in view of his elder brother's constitution, was likely to be king in the early forseeable future. 'Well, Aubrey,' he cried giving his guest a hand as he came aboard, 'you very nearly split the heavens with that damned great rolling broadside – God's my life, thunder and lightning was nothing to compare. Don't I wish you may not have started more than a dozen of your timbers, ha, ha, ha! And don't I wish you may have come by your powder honestly, ha, ha, ha, ha! Allow me to present my young cousin Randolph Miller' – beckoning to a soldier in regimentals, smiling just behind him. 'But of course you know him already, you are neighbours in the country.'

'How do you do, sir?' said Jack, accepting Miller's proffered

[*The manuscript here has been considerably reworked by the author. Pages 101 and 103 (both marked by O'Brian as page 15 of Chapter Three) are different versions of the same material. Page 105 seems to be the later draft, as it corresponds more closely to the typsescript.*]

count two between each shot.'

A profound silence: the target drifted half way down the Surprise's length. 'Fire.' said Jack.

The first gun: and before it quite rang in the second and so close along the line down to the last. When the smoke cleared and the last repeated echo died away there was nothing but tossing water to be seen. The little girls had strength enough to utter a last gasping Oh, and they were led away exhausted: but not before a furious Killick had appeared on the quarterdeck wearing a full-dress coat. 'Which I had it all laid out a quarter of an hour long pad. Ain't you got...' He was going to say 'No shame?' but disapproving looks, coupled with Jack's instant compliance and a call for the barge checked his zeal.

44 With a following breeze and a very well inclined crew the barge fairly skimmed across the sea, looking on only a matter of seconds late. In any case Lord Leyton was in a good mood — he could could be jovial and he could be damned crabbed — but this was a good day. He had heard most of Dr Maturin's acquaintance, close acquaintance, with the Prince William, the Duke of Clarence. who, in view of his elder brother's constitution, was likely to be king in the fairly near future. 'Well Aubrey.' he cried, giving his guest a hand as he came aboard. 'You very nearly split the heavens with that damned great jolly broadside — Gods in my left. thunder and lightning were nothing to compare. Don't I wish you may not have started more than one a dozen of your timbers, he, he, he.! And don't I wish you may have come by your powder honestly, ha, ha, ha, ha.! Allow me to present my young cousin Randolph Miller —.' Beckoning to a soldier in regimentals. standing just behind him —. 'but of course you know him already, you are neighbours in the country...

'How do you do, sir?' said Jack. 'Harry Miller's protégé
 accepting

time between each shot.

A profound silence: the target drifted half way down the Suffolk's length. 'Fire,' said Jack.

The first gun and before it [spent] seen or the second and so clear down to the last: and when the smoke cleared and the last repeated echo died away there were twelve but seven losses write to be seen. The till girls had strength enough to say a last gasping Oh. and then they were led away, exhausted: but not before a furious Killer appeared on the quarterdeck waving a feet drew coat. 'While I heard it all [loud] out a quarter of an hour long past. And you got ...' He was going to say 'no shame.' but disapproving look, coupled with faint compliance and his call for a barge checked his zeal. /44

The barge fairly raced over the smooth water with the meeting tide and they were not perceptibly late, and in any case Lord Leyton, willing to be affable before Dr Maturin, of whose influence with the Duke of Clarence he had heard strange things. greeted them [pleasantly], enough. 'By God, Aubrey.' he said 'you fairly split the heavens with that last rolling boat. Don't I wish you may not have started more than a score of your timbers; and may I ask you came by your powder honestly. he, he, he. Dr Maturin. how do you do, sir? Prince William spoke most kindly of you when last we met. Said you were most uncommon clever. May I name my cousin, Captain Miller — though now I come to think on it, perhaps a physician takes rank over an army officer?'.

'How do you do, sir?' asked Stephen. bowing. And the how do you does were repeated by Jack and Miller and some other guests as they made their way, often giving precedence, to the Admiral splendid. Right they sat down. and with the servants behind each chair they were by no means crowded. Jack, as a flag-officer sat at the Admiral's right. with the Admiral's cousin opposite. 'I

30
11.1
J
0
833

11.1

hand.

'And this, sir, is Dr Maturin, I presume?' said Lord Leyton. 'How kind of you to come. I have had a particular desire to meet you ever since the Duke of Clarence told me you were a most uncommonly learned man. I am not particularly learned myself, but I love to surround myself with those that are. May I introduce you to Captain Miller, my cousin Randolph – but now I come to reflect, perhaps a Doctor of Medicine takes rank over a simple soldier . . .'

'Not at all, my lord: but it so happens that we were at Trinity at much the same time, so I already have that honour.'

'Indeed he was: Trinity College, Dublin. Well then, if he too were at Trinity, then he too is one of the learned – it stands to reason. And I dare say he can split an infinitive as quick as any man. But may I introduce . . .'

Presently they were called to the Admiral's truly splendid dining-cabin, which could seat ten people easily, each with a servant behind his chair and plenty of room for those who came hurrying in with dishes and tureens, sauceboats, trays of bread and of course very large quantities of wine – a grateful Sancerre with the bonito, an Haut-Brion with the admirable duck and an ancient burgundy with the roast beef: unhappily it was corked. The chaplain on Stephen's right murmured something about 'a quaint reminiscence of antiquity' and Jack did not empty his glass; but their host took no notice of his formal first sip and none of his officers showed any sign of awareness. 'Stoicism?' asked Stephen privately. 'Dislike of offending the great man? Discipline? Stark insensibility?'

When it came to the port, however, the case was altered: all hands, including the parson, drank eagerly; and when they reached the loyal toast there was no man who did not drain his brimming glass and murmur, 'God bless him,' with real feeling, and emptied it.

hand.

'And this, sir, is Dr Maturin, I presume?' said LdL. 'How kind of you to come. I have had a particular desire to see you ever since the Duke of Clarence told me that you were a most uncommonly to learned man. I am not particularly learned myself, but I love to surround myself with those that are. May I pre introduce you to my cousin Randolph — but now I come to reflect, perhaps the doctor of medicine takes rank over a soldier...'

'Not at all, my lord: but it so happens that we were at Trinity College together, so I already have that honour.'

'So he was, Trinity College, Dublin. So if he too was at Trinity, he too is one of the learned: it stands to reason. And may I introduce...'

Presently they were called to ~~dinner~~ of the Admiral's truly splendid dining-cabin, which could seat ten people easily, with a servant behind each chair and plenty of room for those who came hurrying in with dishes and tureens, sauceboat, trays of bread, and of course very large quantities of wine — a grateful Sancerre with the bouillo..., with the admiral's duck, and a burgundy of an outlandish year with the roast beef: unhappily, it was corked. The chaplain murmured something about 'a recant odour of antiquity' and Jack did not empty his glass; but their host did not notice his first sip and none of his officers showed any sign of awareness. 'Stoicism?' asked Stephen privately. 'Decline of attendance, great man? Slack insensibility?'

When it came to the port, however, the case was altered: all hands, including the parson, drank eagerly; and when it came to the loyal toast there was no man who did not raise his brimming glass and murmur 'God bless him', with real feeling, having emptied it.

reminiscence

After this ceremony and the chaplain's grace, Lord Leyton observed that although the glass was sinking it was still quite a fine afternoon, and some of them might like to take their coffee, and perhaps some brandy, on deck.

There were general sounds of agreement, a general movement, though with due regard for precedence, and the Admiral keeping Jack by his side until the room was free, said, in answer to his thanks and congratulations, 'Not at all, not at all, my dear fellow – a very simple little feast: though I must admit that they have capital beef in these part. But did you notice anything about the burgundy?'

'No, sir: capital wine.'

'Well, I am glad of that. For a moment I thought – but, however, what I wanted to tell you before coffee was that I should like you to weigh on the ebb and to proceed to Saint Helena under a very easy sail and there to wait in that damned uneasy road-stead until you see me plain. Then you must weigh and carry on for the Cape: there is not room for all three squadrons to lie there safely together in a strong sou'wester. But that will already make a very impressive show of force, I believe.'

'Certainly, sir.'

'And then I should like you to take my nephew along with you. As you may know, he has been given an appointment at the Cape, and the sooner he is there the better – you might even lend him your tender for the last few days, if the wind drops, as it so often does as you approach the coast. Now let us hurry on deck, before all those God-damned soldiers have drunk all the brandy.'

On deck Captain Miller at once came up to Jack and said, 'Sir, I hear with great pleasure that Mrs Aubrey and

After the ceremony and the chaplain's grace, Lord Leyton observed that although the glass was sinking it was still a very fine afternoon, and some of them might like to take their coffee and perhaps some brandy, on deck.

There were general sounds of agreement, a general movement though with due regard to precedence, and the Admiral keeping Jack by his side until the room was free, said, in answer to her thanks and congratulation 'Not at all, not at all, my dear fellow — a very simple little feat. Though I must admit that they have capital bowls here. But did you notice anything about the burgundy?'.

'No, sir: excellent capital wine.'

'Well, I am glad of that. For a moment I thought ... but, however, what I wanted to tell you before coffee is that I should like you to weigh on the ebb and to proceed to St Helen, under a very easy sail, there to wait in that damned uneasy Roadstead until you see me clear of the horizon. Then you must weigh and carry on for the Cape: there is not room for all these of us squadron to lie there safely together in a stiff sou-wester. But that will already make a very impressive show of force.'

'Certainly, sir.'

'And then I should leave you to liase my nephew along with you. As you may know, he unlooks has been given an appointment at the Cape, and the sooner he is there the better — you might even know him, your leader for the last few days. Now let us hurry on deck, before all these God-damned soldiers have drunk all the brandy.'

On deck Captain Miller at once ran up to him and said 'Sir, I hear with great pleasure that Mrs Aubrey and

Mrs Wood are both aboard you, and that perhaps we may be shipmates far as the Cape. Allow me to fetch you a glass of brandy.' Coming back with the glass in his hand he cried, 'My dear cousin has just told me that you will be so very kind as to take me with you. Thank you very much indeed. I did myself the pleasure of waiting on Mr Heatherleigh when he and his sister – whom I already knew and admired from my days in Sierra Leone – were settling at Medenham; and later I called on Mrs Aubrey and Mrs Wood at Woolcombe when you were still at sea – I must congratulate you on your children, sir.'

Jack looked at him with some surprise. Their degree of acquaintance did not warrant anything like this familiarity. 'Has the man drunk too much?' he wondered inwardly: aloud he said, 'Forgive me, if you

[*The first paragraph of the manuscript here was eliminated in the author's typescript version.*]

17A
this will go
at the end of
ms Th.17

To the Cap

'You will carry on, still under a fairly easy sail, and I make no doubt that we shall overtake you a little south of Capricorn — at all events well before Loando, where I mean to put in so that we may all reach the Cape together in full fig. And from that point on I should like you to take my cousin along with you. As you may know, he has an appointment at the Cape, and the sooner he is there the better: you might even lend him your tender for the last few days, so that he can report promptly and snap up one *[?]* the best houses before there is any competition. Now let us hurry on deck, before these God-damned soldiers have drunk all the brandy.'

He moved briskly up the ladder and right aft where a grateful *[?]* of breeze was wafting down to ocean — As soon as Jack had followed him into the open air he was accosted by Akhmev, who took his arm and said 'Sir it is with the greatest pleasure that I hear *[?]* that Mr Aubrey and Mrs Wood are both *[aboard us]*. *[crossed out]* and it is not impossible that perhaps we may be shipmates as far as the Cape.' He came back carrying the brandy and *[?]* so Akhmev *[?]* he cried. 'Yes, my dear cousin tells me that you will be so very kind as to take me with you after the squadron has refreshed at Loando, and I thank you very very much indeed. I did myself the pleasure of waiting on Mr Heatherleigh other *[?]* and his sister — whom I already knew well, and admired. *[crossed out]* from my days in Sierra Leone — we sailing at Medenham; and all later I called on Mrs Aubrey and Mrs Wood at Woolcombe when you were still at sea — I must congratulate you on your children, sir.'

Jack looked at him with some surprise. Their degree of acquaintance did not warrant anything like this familiarity. 'Has the fellow drunk too much?' he wondered inwardly: aloud he said 'Forgive me if you

[margin left, upper:] soldiers though some as cert

*[margin left, lower:] open out *[?]* where it falls in ? the *[?]* down*

please,' and walked across the deck to where Dr Maturin was listening sullenly to Lord Leyton's harangue – his detailed explanation of how he was going to tell Napoleon how he could have avoided defeat at Waterloo. 'Aubrey,' cried Leyton, turning, 'cannot you persuade or even order Dr Maturin to stay while I have my interview with the Emperor – with General Buonaparte, I should say? I can read the French pretty well, with a dictionary at hand, but I cannot speak it with anything like the Doctor's fluency.'

'Oh come, my lord,' said Stephen, 'what you say sounds

[*The typescript ends here.*]

after the
welcome to
to to board

Mrs Wood are both aboard you, and that perhaps we may be shipmates as far as the Cape. Allow me to fetch you a glass of brandy.' He came back carrying it and cried 'Yes. Tho' my dear cousin tells me that you will be so very kind as to lase me with I thank you very, very much indeed. I did myself the pleasure of waiting on Mr Heatherleigh when he and his sister — whom I already knew quite well from my days in Sierra Leone — were settled at Medenham; and a little later I called on Mrs Aubrey and Mrs Wood at Woolcombe when you were still at sea.' I must congratulate you on your children, sir.'

Jack looked at him with some surprise. Their degree of acquaintance did not warrant anything like this familiarity. 'Had the man drunk too much?' he wondered inwardly, and aloud he said 'Forgive me if you please,' and he walked over the deck to where Dr Maturin was listening sullenly to Lord Leyton's harangue — a debate detailed/explanation of how he was going to tell Napoleon how he could have avoided defeat at Waterloo. 'Aubrey,' he cried, turning. 'Cannot you persuade or even order, Dr Maturin to stay until which I have my interview with the Emperor — with Napoleon, I should say. I can read the French pretty well with a dictionary, but I cannot really speak it.'

'Oh come, my lord,' said Stephen. 'What you say sounds very like the French of the northern provinces; and I do assure you I have patients aboard to whom I owe my first duty, to say nothing of what awaits us at the Cape.'

'My lord,' said Jack, 'even an admiral cannot overrule a medical man — it is in the Articles of War — and even if he could he would have no success with Maturin. You may turn a bear from his vomit, but I do solemnly affirm that

the First Lord of the Admiralty could not turn Maturin from his set course, perverse though it may be. But here is my keeper and the barge is alongside: I thank you very heartily indeed for your hospitality, and I shall most willingly carry your nephew to the Cape. Good day to you, my lord. Come, Stephen.

An admiral's barge, though spacious, is still a public place and they said little as they returned to the ship:

No: I shall have to rearrange
these pages on the typewriter

And I must remember to tell the girl
about my missing shoes

If I go back to ∮ TCD I might
look for pen-cartridges

what shall I do with him?

151123
151123

ten beasts of the largest size could not deter Mahon from what he thinks
right. And I do assure you your Lord that when we have some people
on the sick-list in a very parlous state.'

'How do you er mean - pot parlous?'

'Well, my lord, hip and tuck, as you might say, or touch and go.
And it is my impression that as soon as his assistant, Dr Jacob, comes
aboard he means to operate on a strangled hernia.'

'A twisting of the guts, my lord: the poor soul, swelling above because
his shipmates feed him twice at every meal; and he shrunk below. The
patient is a sailmaker's mate.'

'Well, I am sorry for him, but I am sure to have nothing to recommend
but a double handful of small-sho followed by a pint of castor oil.
Yet it is really a medico's business & I shall certainly leave it to. Us
Would it be a very bloody affair?'

'Shockingly so, I fear: though with clips & swabs we shall try to
diminish the flow.'

'I might mention to the Mahon the walking miles to see the castrating of
lambs and bullocks - geldings, for that matter.' The Admiral gave up
of the last sails with unmoved pleasure. 'Now mew at jelly
something like the full T-ads, clear of the land and its turbulences,'
said the Admiral. and [illegible crossed-out lines]
[illegible crossed-out lines]
[illegible crossed-out lines]
[illegible crossed-out lines]
presently he formed the whole South African squadron into the sailing
order, sending his guests back to their ships in the kindest manner.

Truly, once that had sunk the land it was the purest sailing:
nearly 300 miles in his full day, never touching back nor shoal,
and even the Suffolk kept in splendidly. How him wished him
keened navigators Hansen and Hamel. who would so have loved

drawing its almost purely straight lines cutting the parallels at even angles. But how they enjoyed their occasional northern albetross, this not infrequent whales, the almost steady companionship of quite a large variety of shares and even rays!

Jack Or's twins began to grow rather offensively knowledgeable about sea-going affairs but Padeen (to his delight remained strange. uncouth and largely incomprehensible for all finer points) managed to keep them within bounds, and what he could not do Burgos did. It did not make them very pleasant companions but it rendered them tolerable; and the southern coast of Africa and its Portuguese possessions came daily nearer

Miller, who called on the ladies almost every day to suggest ¿ piquet or backgammon (with little success often he whet) was much excited by the prospect of Loando, and he climbed as far as dared to catch a first glimpse of the shore — conceivably a symbol of power, status and indeed perhaps marriage

A dimness on the western horizon, some days, very exact observation of sun, moon, planets, and a wonderfully timely eclipse of one of Jupiter's satellites gave them their line to the minute of ever less

'Now it can come Hell or high water,' said Harding, the Suffolk's first lieutenant and a quartermaster. ~~At~~ Now you know exactly where we are.

He said this in ~~Caplan.~~ the presence of Admiral Saubrey (no mean astronomer himself) who shook his head at the words: so did everyone else in the chartroom. something imperceptibly. But imperceptibly or not, within seconds the sky split with a most enormous roar ~ so prodigious that the twins, well accustomed to sea-born weather, rushed shrieking into their mothers bed.

All night it followed and threatened. St Helena's Fort appearing G or thirty separate mast and the bowsprit three staysails were blown out of the foot-ropes to the fore shrout, and the foretopgallant. With ~~burst~~ infinite pains on a deck that never for a moment stopped flinging

way about about in the most extravagant ~~manner~~, they stowed all that could be stowed and then turned to the pump for the very serious mass of water still below, and to platts swabs and bucket for the knee-deep wet that washed from side to side of the sick-berth. The captain's cabin and the lieutenants ~~store-room~~

A heavy day, night, with nothing to eat but wet biscuit & rum; but it did clear before dawn and rising sun showed not only a beautifully clear but the coast of Loando. with its town and its day. The sea was still grievously troubled and there were half a dozen fishing-boats at least half-wrecked or worse The South African squadron as a whole had ~~been~~ to very early in the night – their topsail were above the horizon, —so Suffolk picked up the fishermen, & lowry their boats carried them into ~~Loando~~, having signalled his intention to the squadron. Loando

They were most lovingly received – many of the fishermen were Hollriver – and they were feasted (though at short notice) in the most splendid, while as for as the exhausted hands were concerned ~~the~~ went down very well indeed. The Admiral commanding squadron was housed in a (rapidly brushed) governors: the / nominal white squadron had no flag-officer at its; but Jack who was after all a rear-admiral of the blue, lived with all his family and senior officers, in the former military command, next to still not inconsiderable barrack

In spite of the shortness of the storm the ships had suffered ~~ext~~ extremely and he, Jack and the other captains were almost perpetually in the well-equipped and capable dockyard. One day, as they were coming back to the Governor house — a shingle strand with singularly coconut palms and their usually birds — Stephen met them and the Admiral asked after his heroic.

'Thank you, sir.' said Stephen. 'he has shown the most remarkable improvement and I think I shall operate in the next two days, now that Jacob is returning. Perhaps I shall mention it to Captain Miller.

'Yes, indeed: he loves medical matters. But it is not particularly

is it?

'Oh, no. Nothing like an amputation. You open intelligently and you are on the job at once.'

'Well. In that case it would be very kind of you, I am sure.'

Stephen came called on the the military headquarters, and walking in he found Miller already there, not to his surprise although it was an almost daily occurrence, but surprising in the way the bunches of flowers had increased and in Christine's marked unfavourable ~~exteins~~ expression

'Oh Captain Miller,' he said, accompanying him to the door, 'I happened to tell the Admiral that I was probably operating upon ~~too~~ favourable her in tomorrow. Should you like to attend?'

'Is it a ~~bloody~~ operation?'

'Oh no. Not what one should really really bloody. If your first incision is badly mistaken it can be somewhat distressing; but we do not commonly mistake.'

'I am sure you do not. But if I may I will excuse myself for these occasions though with many many thanks for your polite attention.'

'Good day to you, sir.'

'Stephen, my dear.' said Christine, 'I am afraid I must beg you ~~till~~ to tell that man not to call unless he is invited. It is becoming quite a nuisance — a wonderfully confident nuisance. It spend a long time in telling in me through all this of breed and tells me that when he had taken up his appointed position at the Cape and when he had married to woman he had chosen there would be virtually nobody in the colony to compete with him in wealth and influence. I have met with some fools in my life. even ~~God damned~~ somehow fools, and a ~~good~~ many of them; but I have never met with such a confident ass as Miller: I suppose he

of completely blinded by his position, appointment and I dare say wealth, as well a gross stupidity. Stephen, please get me rid of him. He is making his detractors as well as himself.

'My dear, I shall attend to.'

It was as soon as when the South African squadron was fit for sea that the Admiral ordered them to sea, there to carry out a very considerable great-gun exercise fairly close in shore to the please view Portuguese friends. The last preparation had not yet taken place before Stephen Maturin met of of Captain Miller. 'O Captain Miller,' he said beside of detaching himself from his friends. 'I have message for you. (lowering his voice) Mrs Wood begs you will not call again with an invitation.' Miller could not a first grasp the meaning, though his complacent smirk did fade. Stephen repeated his words.

'It is not true,' cried Miller. 'Christine never said that.'
'I assure you those were her words.'
'They were not.'
'You give me the lie?' asked Stephen, very low, approaches his face.
'Yes,' cried Miller, and struck him hard. (who had returned a little after midnight)
'You will appoint your friend,' said Stephen. 'These gentlemen —' nodding towards Harding and Joseph, 'will attend to any interests. Good day to you, sir, until early tomorrow morning.' He touched his hat and walked on.

Harding was obliged to leave them to buy some particularly choice handkerchiefs for his wife. and Stephen said 'Oh my dear Jacob, how sorry I am to entangle you with that silly little affair even before you have answered half your questions on your most admirable report of on the Argentine. Shall we have time for a small well-placed uncomplicated heroic before going deeply into practice? I should like to get word of to Sir Joseph directly, since we must sail after early tomorrow afternoon.

'I should imagine so — really both, lea patience with a simple heroic is no great matter and I have already coded the essence of my report. And a simple affair of this kind is no greater matter either: small award a blow given & returned

on the level ground behind the groynes, a little above surgeons, with not a stretcher, his men and a local surgeon. You expect no serious injury?'

'No. A pierced shoulder at the most.'

'Very well. Let us look at our patient & perhaps operate at once, or at the £ cost of landing him until the exercise is over.'

In fact, although the operation went perfectly well. The man Hainer was landed — at the Admiral's particular request, on two grounds: the first that it stood to reason some gun or other — would burst or overset, and second. that the roaring of broadsides — arouse his feeling & excite the blood; whereas on shore he would be perfectly calm and _____ under Mrs Aubrey; & Mr Wood's care.

But the Admiral was worried, very much more worried. by his nephews adverse in the morning and by the rumours. brought by the Admiral's secretary that Miller had flatly refused to fight with _____ He would pistol or he would not fight. Maturin seconds would have none of it: it was their principal who had been struck — it was he who chose the weapons. That was always the same: it always had been the case. It was the Law of Moses.

'Of course it is.' said the Admiral. 'I always preferred the gentleman's weapon who I went out: except when I was the aggressor and had to take the other man's choice — Pray. Mr Martin.' he went on. 'pray turn out & see if you can catch them. Tell him privately from me that if he don't fight he is disgraced for ____ & can expect no notice from me — no from the Ministry ⊙ And tell me a sword wound wound given by a reasonably decent creature is not so wicked. particularly if you dress it with marshmallow and heartsease.'

the far v end

On the field. from which so curious onlookers had been shooed with appalling violence, the scene was only just not ridiculous Miller had been urged forward by his seconds and he kept telling them that it was perfectly unfair — he knew everything about pistols: he would meet any man with a pistol. But he knew nothing about swords

They, stone-faced, kept telling him it was the law of the duel. He could either apologize on his knees, using any terms his adversary saw fit to impose, or he must fight. There was no true ways about. Mr Martin whispered into his ear "Your uncle will not speak to you if you do not fight."

They thrust a sword into his hand, pointed toward that of his adversary. The chief second held them on his outstretched blade. Cried 'Gentlemen, engage,' and strode back.

Two, three or even four clashes, and Miller's flew out to act. It landed between them. Stephen put his foot on it and his sword-point against. 'Do you withdraw?' he asked. 'Miller, do you withdraw your words entirely?' 'I do. Entirely.'

'Yes?. Then we have said enough. Good day to you, gentlemen, and I thank you for your presence.'

'He spoke smeared all with a set of tools,' said Wainwright into Killick's eager ear. He was Miller's servant and he cordially disliked his master; but since he was a child and grandchild of Cockley Horn he had learnt to express himself in gentler expression — not that their kind had any currency whatsoever with Killick or mine. Tenths of the lower deck.

'Where does he stow himself now?'

'Why, in the little cabin behind his lordship; and I doubt he comes out so soon. It is fair wonderful what a face of brass will do, but I doubt anyone could face the country — the English country, the part around us, or in London — having as he were as damned refused to fight. I remember how his lordship went out half-dozen times when I was young — and always bloodied his sword... Come, sir,' he cried, and vanished aft.

Killick delighted in pineapple-shrub and in pigs' trotters; but they did not nearly reach his high and exalted pleasure in very specifically obscene (which alas he could never remember accurately or even at all) stories, however improbable) and accounts of high life.

25

He did not come on deck. the next day. that of the ~~previous~~ prodigious, ~~very~~ heavy great-gun exercise; nor did he appear for the small. arm excise. in which he had trained some of the Mariners From time to time he turned into the ward-room, when almost nobody was there. — His appearance never altered ~~perpetually~~ [to pick up a newspaper] from its pimpled smallpox complexion, yet he frequently changed his uniform, being perpetually strained for any hop

Some days of such unexpected ~~Saspice St~~ St Atrecs ~~upsetter~~ weather showed the squadron and ~~it was possibly during these hours~~ ~~sitting in the cabin that~~ —— possible and it was well have been during the conversation

No: there is such a lot of III — LoL's dinner or part of it — missing

It is not in the MS broken: but I remember now that there was.

I also - plan at the course change

Alas. I cannot find it: lost pages. have lost of MS chapters
are the almost daily bane of my life: could there be a
malignant hand?

In this case I may be able to rebuild the odd pages: but
I shall have to first and concentrate what units I still possess

← JA pulls agi across barely leb

LoL big elderly interested jovial 'split the heavens'
interested in SM's friendship with Clarence — transmit praise
— present Capt Miller 'my cousin

'een' Miller over-familiar comes out Message Jacob ? almost
I think (seating) at coffee is which Dr J is aboard
 pretty spry but rather worn

LoL

JA ⌐ ⌐ Miller
 Flag capt
Senior RM ⊢
(Col? Major)

SM ⊢ ⊢

Dr W ⊢ ⌐
 Chaplain

afterwards privately
LoL asks JA to
proceed to St Helene
under easy sail, Taking Miller
(who has an appointment
appointment at th Cape) & to
lie off in th indifferent holding ground
& as soon as sails are seen to weigh
(show of force)
perhaps as some of the squadron
are dull sailers Miller might be lent
tender (? name)

just read through for
names of ships

& work out Suffolk's
wardroom

AFTERWORD

by Richard Snow

THE OTHER DAY I heard Patrick O'Brian receive about as high a compliment as a writer can get. An old friend of mine, a professor of history and literature, had just read *Master and Commander* again for the first time in a decade. "How well it holds up!" he exclaimed. "It's amazing. That first meeting, it's like – " He waved his hand as he searched for a comparison. "It's like Prince Hal meeting Falstaff."

The meeting, of course, takes place between Lieutenant (for just a few more hours) Aubrey, and a weedy-looking little physician named Maturin. It was a contentious meeting, and might well have led swiftly to the death of one of the two – most likely the young naval officer. Instead, of course, it led to the greatest friendship of modern literature, and ushered millions of twentieth-century citizens into a world warmed and clouded by sea-coal fire, rationalized and tormented by the architects of the Enlightenment, fed salvers of steaming offal washed down with suicidal quantities of claret and port, and defended by hundreds of close-packed seaborne towns whose elders' grasp of mathematics, physics, ballistics, and meteorology was all that stood between the residents and extinction.

My friend who made the Shakeseare comparison, Fredric Smoler, had come early to this harsh, seductive world, back when its creator's books were struggling to find an audience in the United States. Lippincott, Stein & Day, *Master and Commander*, *Post Captain*, *HMS Surprise* . . . the publishers tried and withdrew – after *Desolation Island*, permanently. Or so it seemed. During the years of drought, Patrick O'Brian's acolytes did what they could to keep Jack Aubrey and Stephen Maturin in their lives. They opened accounts at the great English bookstore Hatchards; they wrote to booksellers in Canada; the most fortunate of them acquired, along with the precious novels, a correspondence with the lively and generous-spirited Richard Ollard, O'Brian's English editor, and himself a formidably accomplished historian and a superb writer. Another friend of mine, the journalist Mark Horowitz (who would later publish an influential profile of Patrick O'Brian in the *New York Times Magazine*), had left New York to become a belligerently loyal Angeleno, and sent Fred and me messages saying that every bookshop in Los Angeles stocked imported O'Brian novels – and how do you like that, you haughty Manhattanites? (Surely this can't have been entirely true, and yet Mark always seemed to have read the latest one before we did.) In the meantime, of course, we proselytized, with the predictable success:

Them: I've read all the Hornblower novels, and that's enough for me.

Us: But that's like saying, I've read *Robinson Crusoe* so there's no reason for me to look at Dickens.

Such harangues often ended with an indulgent smirk from the victim. And why not? If this writer was really all that good, everybody would know about him, right?

It's a fair question, and eventually Starling Lawrence answered it. He is the editor-in-chief of W. W. Norton & Company, and in 1990 O'Brian's agent, Vivien Green, pressed a copy of *The Reverse of the Medal* on him as he was leaving London bound for New York. By the time he disembarked at JFK he had been won over: he would bring out the next O'Brian, *The Letter of Marque*. This was a courageous decision; the series had already failed here, and it is considerably more costly to publish a writer than it is to pester your friends about him across a dinner table.

But it turned out to be the right time. All those scattered little enclaves glowing with O'Brian enthusiasm were ready to reach combustion. The resulting blaze created rather than destroyed; so far it has cooked up five million copies and an admirable motion picture that will continue to spread the word for years to come. (That the movie became the object of some prissy reproach for not more fully unfurling the characters of Stephen and Jack only ratifies the power of the books that gave it birth.) This American enthusiasm sent ripples back across the Atlantic. On a visit to London in the mid-1990s, I was gratified to see that O'Brian's novels had been moved out of "Naval Fiction," a bookstore section we alas don't have over here, across the aisle into "Literature."

So in a very short time everybody finally did know about Patrick O'Brian, to a degree that when he visited our shores he attracted a following of a dedication and willingness to travel great distances to be in The Presence that seems to me equaled only by that of the Grateful Dead or the Rolling Stones. And, like Mick Jagger, he never disappointed. What writer since Hemingway – and perhaps Fitzgerald – has looked so thoroughly the way you'd want him to? Clean-shaven, slim, slightly below middle height but giving the impression of that "wiry strength" more often found in novels than on the speaker's podium, and with the affect of bemusement that was, I think, a sort of courtesy to soften the impact of those daunting eyebrows and the comprehension, wit, and, occasionally, caustic scorn that flicked from him unceasingly. And then he was gone. Gone not merely from New York and Los Angeles and Seattle and all the other cities where people of high consequence were now wild to get him to their dinner parties, but from the world.

AND YET, as the surprising volume you are holding reminds us, he is not gone at all. When death took Patrick O'Brian, this book had not been given a name. It had advanced only three chapters, 65 handwritten pages, most of which had been typed and given preliminary corrections by O'Brian (I say "preliminary" because there are, here and there, a few repetitions that this most scrupulous of writers would not have permitted himself). O'Brian in holograph offers advantages and drawbacks. I find his handwriting both exquisite and difficult to read, but persevering through it offers the pleasures of a wonderful bloodless duel that Stephen engineers, and a casual sketch of a seating arrangement that has the electrifying effect of making the principals seem entirely like living people. "21" is a fragment, of course, and one would expect such a document to be little more than a forlorn remnant. After all, O'Brian had been composing it during a melancholy time. His wife, Mary, had died; he was alone; he was eighty-five years old; and his newfound fame had brought his life under media

scrutiny that would have dismayed people far less protective of their privacy than he.

But just look at "21"! There is no sense of harassment or desolation here, no loss of focus, nor of energy. And if it ends too soon, it is nonetheless a rich distillation – a summary of sorts – of all that has, over thousands of pages and tens of thousands of miles, won O'Brian such passionate admirers. First of all, there is the language – and here I mean not O'Brian's prose but what he gives his characters to say. He insisted that their speech was an accurate reflection of how early nineteenth-century people talked; but I believe it is a brilliant poetic invention, complex yet so wholly consistent that we in time learn to speak it almost through the same process we would follow acquiring a foreign language. It never ceases to show us that this is a world at once remote and familiar, and the conveying of that familiarity is, I think, a feat of the imagination that far surpasses, say, J. R. R. Tolkien's kingdoms of dwarfs and sorcerers.

We get to be introduced to Jack and Stephen one last time, and how keen the pleasure remains: Stephen abashed in the composition of his heavily-coded love letter; Jack with elephantine, ignorant delicacy discussing the Church of Rome with his closest friend. And here is Killick, his insolence for once extinguished by the calamity that has befallen Jack's best uniform during freezing weeks off the Horn. Now come the curiously stirring details: the men begging slush from the galley to give the shot in the garlands a pleasing sheen; Stephen clipping the tip of his pen "with a minute pair of metal jaws made for the purpose." To be sure, there's no battle in these pages, but the great-gun exercise on the Sussex gives a highly satisfactory sense of the violence and power that men like Jack Aubrey controlled. And any disappointment at the lack of a frigate duel must be eradicated by the presence of the humor that quietly leavens every paragraph. Jack, explaining how he acquired the extra gunpowder necessary for his spectacular exercise, says he'd bribed "the last powder-hoy, for a trifle of whiskey – you know the Irish drink, Stephen, I am sure?" "I have never heard of it," says Stephen. This tiny exchange is marvelously appealing: both men are being funny; both men understand one another perfectly.

Their amity suggests what I find so moving about this last work from Patrick O'Brian's hand. Some of the novels end with their principals settled and content, some with them in poverty and peril. It is, of course, impossible to say where "21" would have left them. I'm sure the egregious Captain Miller would have reappeared to work some malice after Stephen's humiliation of him. And Jack's money-making initiatives would likely have put him on the metaphorical lee-shore.

Right now, however, we are able to visit these friends we have followed so very far in a rare state of almost perfect felicity. Jack has seen his black son ably discharging important duties. Sophie and his daughters are with him; Brigid is with her father, she's thriving, and Stephen is with a woman who is very dear to him. Jack is flying a rear-admiral's flag aboard a ship of the line. So we can leave them sailing through fair, sweet days – Stephen with his dissections, Jack with his "sacred blue flag," Killick muttering darkly over the toasted cheese – embarked on a voyage like the one that opens the book: "Quietly indeed they sailed along, with gentle breezes that wafted them generally northwards at something in the nature of five miles in the hour, north-

wards to even warmer seas. Little activity was called for, apart from the nice adjustment of the sails, and although the exact routine of the ship was never relaxed nor her very strict rules of cleanliness, these long sunny days with a soldier's wind seemed to many the ideal of a seaman's life – regular, steady, traditional meals with the exact allowance of grog; hornpipes in the last dog-watch, the deep melody of the Doctor's 'cello from the cabin and the cheerful sound of the gunroom's dinner; the future lost in a haze somewhere north of the equator."

Remember that this was written at a time when the author was lonely and tormented. Yet Patrick O'Brian has given a farewell to his followers that is as gracious as it is gallant. And we, in turn, may find some solace in the thought that of all people, this man would not have hated to be taken out of action much as Nelson was: deep in triumph, shedding glory on the service he loved, and still at the peak of his powers.